The Doctor Comes Home

by Samuel To

The Doctor Comes Home
© 1993 by Samuel To

Publisher and Distributor:
Peacock Enterprises
10333 Lundene Drive
Whittier, CA 90601-2032
U.S.A.

ISBN 0-937673-09-9

Printed in the United States of America

Table of Contents

Names and Places In Chinese

Jesus　耶　穌

SO To-Ming　蘇　道　明

TO To-Ming　杜　道　明

　To-Ming's Nickname, Tseng-Po　曾　保

　To-Ming's wife, Pong　龐

FRIENDS:
Leung Chu-Sun　梁　柱　臣

Leung Yee-Fung　梁　夷　風

Ou Fung-Chao　區　鳳　墀

Ouyang Shing-Chack　區　陽　聖　澤

Tsui Shing-Cheung　徐　成　章

PLACES:
Kim-Lee　金　利

Sun-Kiu　新　橋

Yiu-Koo　要　古

Sam-Shui　三　水

Gum San (Gold Mountain, America)　金　山

Bamboo Island　竹　州

About The Author

Samuel To received B.S., M.S. (Chemical Engineering), and Ph.D.(Environmental Engineering) degrees from Virginia Polytechnic Institute and State University (1974). Responding to the call for full-time ministry, he completed a Master's degree from Capital Bible Seminary in 1990.

For 17 years Samuel worked as an environmental engineer, including 12 years in the U.S. Environmental Protection Agency, managing national environmental programs.

He served as an elder at the Chinese Bible Church of Maryland for 15 years. In March 1991, he answered the call to be pastor of the church's branch in College Park, near the University of Maryland.

During his engineering career he published articles in such national publications as *Journal of Colloid* and *Interface Science, Journal of WPCF, American Standard Testing Materials*, and others. He also gave papers and led workshops sponsored by the American Institute of Chemical Engineers, U.S. Environmental Protection Agency, and Water Pollution Control Federation.

In addition, he has published articles in Chinese Christian publications such as the *Ambassador* and the *Challenger*. He leads workshops for organizations such as Chinese Missions 92 and the Greater Washington Christian Education Convention.

Endorsement

Reading this book will fascinate you with God's grace in one man's life. From being a child beggar in China, becoming a Christian in America, becoming a medical doctor, and being reunited with his family, this story is as exciting as that of Joseph in the Old Testament. The story is a wonderful testimony of how God does indeed "work all things together for good to them that love God."

As you follow the journey of TO To-Ming, you will see his life intersect with important historical events of modern China: the end of the Ching Dynasty, the Taiping Rebellion, and the life of Dr. Sun Yat-Sen.

Rev. John Tung
Assistant Minister
Chinese Bible Church of Maryland
Rockville, Maryland

Foreword

Samuel To is my brother, co-worker, and fellow soldier in the Lord. His spiritual growth, ordination as an elder, and entrance into full-time ministry have brought immense joy to my life. Indeed, God's election and work in a person's life is marvelous.

As I read Samuel's biography of his great-grandfather and of the great-grandfather's attempt to trace his roots, I realized that God's mystery is made known to us through simple things when we come to Him with simplicity and humility.

"God's sovereignty (rule) and man's agency" is a profound theological doctrine. But, if viewed in the life of TO To-Ming, it can be easily understood. Although what To-Ming encountered in life can be viewed as misfortunes from a human perspective, God's sovereign hand was behind everything. He was in control. God brought To-Ming to the United States through unpleasant circumstances so that His purposes could be accomplished in TO's life. I am reminded of Joseph's encounters recorded in the Old Testament. Joseph's words to his brothers were, "I am your brother, Joseph, whom you sold into Egypt. And now do not be grieved or angry with yourselves, because you sold me here; for God sent me before you to preserve life." (Genesis 45:4-5).

May God use this book to strengthen our Christian faith, especially the faith of those who are living under adverse circumstances.

Dr. Fred T. Cheung
Pastor,
Chinese Evangelical Free Church
Monterey Park, California

Preface

There are many similarities between the ancient Chinese and the old Hebrew cultures. One of them is attaching significance to personal names. Often, names are chosen for their meaning or to commemorate a special occasion.

There are more than six thousand surnames among the Chinese. Most people know of the common ones such as Chans, Wongs, and Lees. Few people know of the TOs. TO, a rather unusual surname, comes with a more unusual story.

The story started with Dr. TO To-Ming (1845-1919), my great grandfather.[1] From childhood to adulthood, he experienced unusual blessings in the midst of difficult periods. He attributed the blessings to God. He saw benefit in the tough times because he believed that "...God causes all things to work together for good to those who love God..." (Romans 8:28).

The story of my great grandfather's experience touched me from the time I was a little child. I am indebted to my parents who told me his story when I was about six. I am also indebted to my mother for hand-copying both the testimony and the TO genealogy that were recorded by my great grandfather. Many of the details in this book were based on her hand-copied documents.

For years after I first heard the story, I wanted to find out more details. I started to compile the material in 1972, while

---

[1] The Chinese names for people in this book are listed with surname first to conform to the standard Chinese usage, and the Wade-Giles System for Chinese names. Often, the translation (or transliteration) conforms to the Cantonese pronunciation which was the common dialect in Southern China, as well as the majority of Chinese immigrants in America. (For example, the well known American Chinese food, "chow mien," is Cantonese.) In addition, the surname "TO" is capitalized to differentiate it from the "To" in the first name "To-Ming."

working on my doctoral research in Virginia. Through the years, I was overjoyed to find other materials, such as biographies of the Christians that helped To-Ming, that corroborated the details of the story. Materials gathered included books, articles, letters, pictures, and conversations with people who knew my great-grandfather. Materials were found in English and Chinese, and gathered from Hong Kong, Canton and San Francisco.

Through the years, I have shared this story with my relatives and friends. In 1972, I started writing it down and collecting background materials. In recent years, completing the manuscript took on a higher priority as I began to realize that my children might not be as fluent as I am in both Chinese and English. Many of the source documents were written in Chinese, including classical Chinese, and I was concerned that my children might not be able to continue the task of correlating the material.

Chinese like to bring glory to their family name. My intention, in writing this book, goes beyond Chinese culture, in that I want God's name to be glorified. In a way this is a story about my name, but it is really a story of a life changed through knowing Christ. I trust that many readers will also experience the same God who continues to change lives throughout the centuries.

People often search for meaning in life, trying to find out where they came from and where they are going. Sometimes, children of immigrants venture to the land of their forefathers in Africa, Europe or Asia to seek their sense of identity. To-Ming, the main character, found his true identity. Not only did he find his physical roots, he also found his spiritual roots in God, which in turn affected his eternal destiny.

This book includes accounts about early immigrants to the West Coast in America. During their stay in America, many became Christians. This book is written with a prayer that America would continue to be a place where people of all races can come to find special meaning and purpose for their lives.

This book also offers a glimpse of the life of Christians in China in the last century. They were a minority in a land where Christianity is viewed as a foreign religion. I was deeply moved by their dedication and seriousness in teaching the truth. Their faith was tested and challenged as they lived out their faith in all aspects of their lives.

This book is also a tribute to the Christians who understood the implication of Christianity and shared blessings with people around them. These Christians even extended their outreach to despised racial minorities and sojourners in their own country. It was only in recent decades that missiologists have promoted the importance of reaching the "hidden people" groups left out because they were separated culturally, linguistically or socially from others in the same country. In this biography, we find that the American Presbyterian missionaries had reached out to a "hidden people" decades before this concept became popular.

Heartfelt appreciation is expressed to the following people: Linda Leung Chan, a cousin who spent much time in the early 1970's locating pertinent information from the San Francisco area; Ai-Mei Du Yu, my cousin, who provided pictures of the village in China in 1988; Amy To Chan, my sister, for helping with some sketches, other relatives who provided relevant information; Priscilla Saint, Ren Yao, Becky Fong, Rev. John Tung and Wilberta Chinn for reviewing the draft and offering valuable suggestions; and my wife Winnie, daughters, Josephine, Priscilla, and Isabel, for encouraging me and praying for me in writing this book.

CHAPTER 1
Tough Childhood

"...you meant evil against me, but God meant it for good..."
Genesis 50:20

Ming was born in a village, about fifty miles west of Canton, near the delta of the Pearl River. Like many of the small villages in Southern China, it was a cluster of houses of a few family clans, surrounded by acres of farms, rice paddy fields or fishponds.

Several houses were connected by stone paths. Most of these houses were small and simple. There were also a few bigger houses for large households that had close relatives living together.

With so many relatives as neighbors, Ming had to learn to address each one by his or her distinct titles. As with other Chinese children, learning to address and respect the older generation was considered the beginning of maturity. In the Western culture, these relationships are only generally termed "Uncle" or "Aunt". The Chinese culture distinguishes relationships by blood and marriage lines.[2] These titles define the position of members within the family hierarchy and determine each member's obligation within the family. Addressing relatives, especially older people, by their proper

---

[2] The Chinese place great emphasis on family relationships. Dr. Donald McGavran, a well-known missiologist, explained in his book, *Understanding Church Growth*, the importance of understanding the Chinese kinship system in reaching Chinese (pp. 185-186). He cited the need to know about 75 terms for the different relationships. Actually, there are over a hundred such terms or titles. As mentioned before, obligations in the family also come with the titles of relatives.

titles indicated respect. If Ming did not know the exact titles, he could copy the example of his cousins of the same age.

As a toddler, Ming was frequently carried in his father's arms, held close to his bosom. His father usually sat by the door of the house. That was Ming's only recollection of his father since his father died when he was only three or four years old.

After his father's death, his mother had no livelihood, so she remarried. Since his uncle and aunt did not want to take care of him, she took him along to her new home. Like many of the parents in Southern China, she carried her child on her back with a cloth child-carrier while doing her chores or talking to relatives.

One night, Ming dreamed that someone had come to beat him. He was very scared and cried, and did not want to stay in that new home. So, his mother took Ming back to her own mother so he could be cared for. He addressed his new caretaker as "Po-Po," a term for maternal grandmother in Chinese.

Later, Ming's paternal grandfather learned about Ming's situation. His paternal grandfather told others, "Ming is my only grandchild. How can I let other people take him away and then treat him like that?" So he went to Ming's maternal grandmother to negotiate for the custody of Ming.

As a result, Ming's paternal grandparents brought him back to his own village. Living with his paternal grandparents was far from luxurious. They were weak and very poor, but they took good care of him. His paternal grandmother spun cotton to provide additional support for the family.

His uncle and other relatives also took turns providing food for Ming's grandparents, about ten days each. Thus, Ming indirectly benefited from the caring his grandparents received from his relatives. For instance, wherever his grandparents went, Ming was taken along. This way, whenever his grandparents ate in a relative's house, Ming could eat with them. At night, he slept with his grandfather. For another year and a half, he suffered neither hunger nor cold.

Good times, however, did not last long. Both paternal grandparents died within a short time, and he was left alone to fend for himself. He stayed alone in his father's old house. No adults came to help him comb his hair, wash his face, or to prepare his food. Once in a while, different relatives would still give him meals, but their attitude changed drastically from the time when his grandparents were alive. Even though they were aware of his predicament and his suffering from hunger and cold weather, they often ignored him. Even Uncle Hon-Chin, his father's only brother, refused to provide food for him.

One day, he was very hungry. Not knowing when and how the next meal would come, he became desperate. He decided to visit his Po-Po's home to see whether he could get a meal. He remembered the name of her village and found out how to get there. To get to her house, he had to pass through town, and then walk on the dike on the other side of town. The distance was about two miles. For a six or seven year old, the lonely trek through the winding dirt path would be quite tiring. However, memory of Po-Po's kindness motivated him to believe that even a simple meal would be worth the long trip.

Gathering courage, Ming walked outside the village gate. On the path outside the village, he met Uncle Hon-Chin coming back from the market. Recognizing that Ming was taking a special trip, Uncle Hon-Chin asked with a stern voice, "Nephew Ming, what are you doing so far away from our village?"

"I just want to go and visit Po-Po."

On hearing that, Uncle Hon-Chin became very angry. He probably did not want other relatives to know that he was mistreating his nephew. He smacked Ming's face. His blow was so hard that Ming fell to the ground. Ming cried and pleaded, but it was no use. Uncle Hon-Chin still would not permit him to visit his maternal grandmother's home.

CHAPTER 2
The Taiping Rebellion

When Ming was about six years old, the Taiping Rebellion ravaged much of Southern China. It sought to replace the Ching Dynasty with a new dynasty, called Taiping (literally "Great Peace") Heavenly Kingdom.

Three hundred years earlier (in 1644), the Manchu warriors north-east of China had marched south and conquered the Chinese empire, starting the Ching Dynasty. Considered barbarians by the native Han Chinese, the Manchus had distinctly different language and culture. Even the Great Wall, which was built to keep out barbarians from the north, could not keep the superior Manchu warriors out. Similar to many races that entered China before them, the Manchus, who came in as rulers, were assimilated into the native Han Chinese culture.

Throughout the three hundred years, many attempted to overthrow the Ching Dynasty. Besides resenting the rule by foreigners, centuries of ruthless suppression by the Ching Dynasty were hard for the Han Chinese to forget. For instance, the pigtail, the infamous hair style for men, had been imposed by the Manchus after they conquered the Han Chinese in 1640's. Refusing the pigtail was a sign of rebellion, for which the penalty was severe. Only the Buddhist monks, whose religious practice required that they shave their heads, were exempted from the pigtail.

The Taiping Rebellion was started in 1851 by Hung Siu-Chuan, who was born in the nearby Flower County, less than fifty miles from Ming's village. Due to the corruption of the Ching Dynasty, and the harsh treatment of the majority Han Chinese, Hung was able to rally the support of his fellow Hans in Southern China. Thus, in less than three years, his army advanced a thousand miles to the north. In 1853, he established the capital of the Taiping Heavenly Kingdom at Nanking, a major city near the estuary of the Yangtze River.

Hung first learned about Christianity in 1836, when he read a Christian booklet from Leung A-Fah[3] while he was taking a literary examination in Canton. In 1847, he and his cousin returned to Canton to study about Christianity under Issachar Jacox Roberts, a Southern Baptist missionary. He was probably serious about Christianity because he went back to study under Roberts for another two months. Although Hung was impressed by Christianity and learned some principles and features of the Christian religion, he apparently did not become a Christian. Instead, he promoted his own brand of religion, with just superficial resemblances to Christianity. Using this new religion as a unifying force, he mustered enough support to overthrow the Ching Dynasty. Even though he passed out Bibles and attempted to use Christians, his rebellion brought a mixed bag of benefits and sufferings to China.

A bright side to Hung's rule, especially in the beginning, was his zeal to purge evils of the day. He discouraged the worshiping of idols. His reign banned many corrupt practices of the day, such as prostitution, opium smoking, foot-binding for young girls, gambling, etc. His rebellion inspired future revolutions, such as by Dr. Sun Yet-Sen.

Yet, his revolution also had a dark side. Like many emperors before him, Hung kept a harem, and his regime was quite brutal in executions. Hung did not accept the advice of Christians to reform his understanding of Christianity. As a result, he taught distorted versions of some of the cardinal doctrines of Christianity. Because of Hung's conflicting claims and his twisted practice of Christianity, opinions of Westerners (including missionaries) towards the rebellion ranged from ambivalence to skepticism.

---

[3] Leung was a convert of Robert Morrison, the first Protestant Missionary to China.

Later, the over-zealousness of Taiping armies angered many people. For instance, in their zeal to wipe out idols, they sought out Buddhist temples, destroyed statutes and dispersed monks. Wiping out Buddhist practices, which had been respected in China for centuries, alienated many devotees. Sometimes, they even destroyed statues of Mary in many Catholic churches. Such practices angered the French government and the Catholic Church. Thus, initial support from foreign countries shifted to the Ching Dynasty. Weakened support from native Chinese and foreign governments led to the downfall of the Taiping Rebellion (which was later completely wiped out in 1864). Yet, in the intervening years, the rebellion and its subsequent suppression laid waste to much of Southern China.

Even the good reports of the Taiping Rebellion did not help inhabitants in Ming's area. Taiping rebel soldiers were like bandits, looting the homes of the common folks. Homes in Ming's village were likewise affected. One time, Taiping soldiers came to his village to loot, to burn houses, and to kidnap people. Seeing their arrival, villagers started to run for safety. Being so young, Ming wondered what the fleeing was all about. Fortunately, a few older paternal cousins saw him. They grabbed him into a small boat and rowed to the middle of the pond in front of the village. Since the bandits had no way of getting to the middle of the pond, Ming and his cousins were saved from any harm.

While the Taiping Rebellion raged, the economic situation got worse. Ming's relatives became more reluctant to offer him meals. Later, as the Ching Dynasty routed out the Taiping rebellion, the lives of common people got even harder. By then, his uncle completely refused to give meals to him anymore. Even his distant aunts, who used to offer some left over food once in a while, also refused to feed him.

One day, Ming was very cold and hungry. With no one to depend on, he wondered what he should do. He thought again about Po-Po, his maternal grandmother, who had been very kind to him in the past. Even though she lived a few miles away, she seemed his last hope for help. Surely, since his uncle had refused to feed him, he wouldn't prevent Ming from visiting Po-Po. So he started his long trek to her village, hoping to find more food. Arriving at her village, he was surprised to hear crying from many people inside the house. He wondered what had happened. He saw Po-Po crying, with tears covering her face.

She held him by the hand, patted him on the shoulder and said, "It's not the same any more, your uncle (mother's brother) died. Having been falsely accused of helping the Taiping Rebellion, he was executed by Ching officials. So it may be better for you to leave quickly. Please don't come again. Now that your uncle is dead, we can't provide for you anymore."

She gave him a few pounds of rice, and bade a friend to accompany him back to his own village. Knowing that he might not see her again, he cried all the way home. His uncle's death and Po-Po's sorrow only added to his sadness. With his last dependable source of help from relatives gone he knew that he had to start fending for himself.

He had two alternatives for survival. He could ask for left-over food from relatives or he could go begging in town. With no more support from relatives, he was forced to beg until the day he was abducted at about seven or eight years of age.

CHAPTER 3
Kidnapped And Sold

"And we know that God causes all things to work together for good to those who love God, to those who are the called according to His purpose."

Romans 8:28

In addition to begging, Ming received a few scraps of food from relatives. Once in a while, a distant aunt would give him enough left-overs to last a couple of days. Other times, some kind relatives would give him a handful of rice grains.

His routine included a long walk around the village. After other people's mealtime, he would go around to collect the left-overs. Then, he strolled back along the little stone path leading to his house. Sitting down on an old chair, he would eat the food he had collected.

Unlike the left-over food, eating rice grains was not as easy. The rice had to be cooked. For a seven year old, however, cooking was not an easy task. He would need water, clean rice, the right proportion of water, and a fire. He had to fetch water from the creek with a small bucket. To get cleaner water from the well that was farther away, he needed the help of bigger cousins. To prepare the rice, he put a small bowl with the grains into a clay pot. He washed the rice a few times to remove sand and dirt. Since rice grains were threshed on the ground, sand and dirt were often mixed in with the rice. Cooking rice with too little water would lead to a charred crust of burnt rice at the bottom of the pot. To safeguard any loss of precious rice, Ming often put in extra water to be safe.

For the fire, he gathered twigs and wood chips. He put them inside a small clay stove behind the house. After starting the fire and fanning the flame, he would put the pot on the clay stove to cook the rice. Keeping watch was important to avoid boiling over and overcooking.

In the 1850's, a famine affected people throughout Southern China. Food, even left-over, became a rare commodity. As a result, even the meager supply from Ming's relatives stopped coming.

One day, after walking around the village, he came back to his house empty handed. Earlier that morning, he had just finished his last dish of food. Hunger pangs growling from his stomach, Ming knew that he had to find some food. Consequently, he decided to go begging in the nearby marketplace, about a mile away. From then on, rain or shine, he would trek to the town, begging from morning till evening. During storms, he would take shelter in the small temple near the marketplace.

Ming's primary targets were the rice shops on the street next to the main temple in the town. The lane was called the Righteous Lane. Every morning, he would make his round of begging around those shops. Standing in front of the shops, he would ask for a few small handfuls of rice.

Some shopkeepers were not congenial to this ragged little boy. Daily, he encountered the common response, "Please go next door! We have to do business. We can't have little beggars in front of the door." This was the traditional way of politely asking beggars to leave.

In those tough days, pleasant incidents were rare. A few kind men, however, left indelible impressions on Ming's mind. Shopkeepers of one rice store were unusually kind. They never yelled at Ming, nor refused him rice. Whenever Ming passed by, they would give him extra handfuls of rice, enough for one meal.

Another kind man was a merchant he encountered on a dreary, cold market day. On market days (like a county fair), villagers gathered at the market to sell their produce, providing good opportunities to beg and collect food scraps. On this day, however, the cold weather kept many villagers at home. While begging on the road near the river, a heavy storm caught Ming outside, soaking him to the skin. He felt the chill from the storm and was shivering. Soon, his stomach began to cramp. His worn-out clothes provided little protection from the elements. Holding his hands to his aching stomach, he curled up by the road side. Thinking that nobody knew or cared about his pain, he wept. A merchant standing on a cargo junk near the shore, noticed Ming's predicament. The merchant jumped onto shore and walked to him. Reaching into his pocket, the merchant took out about twenty copper coins and placed them in Ming's hand.

For a few more months, Ming continued begging, until he was about seven or eight. One day, while Ming was walking by the big tree by the village entrance, an unfamiliar woman grabbed him by the arm and abducted him. Not knowing this stranger, he tried to free himself from her grip. The strength of a hungry boy was no match for this woman. Even as she dragged him through the streets of town, no one came to his rescue. Few people in town knew him. Furthermore, to a passer-by, the scenc was just like a mean mother dragging her son along.

Not wanting to go, he cried all the way. As he was being dragged along, the woman said that she would gct him a better life. Trying to be nice, she even took out a few copper coins, stopped by a street-vendor to buy some cakes, and then put them in his hands for him to fill his empty stomach. She took him to the river bank, and they got on a ferry boat and traveled downstream.

CHAPTER 4
Sold Into Captivity

After the abduction, the woman took Ming to the river bank by the town. They got on a boat. The next day, they arrived at a big town on the Pearl River delta. This was the first time that he had ever seen so many big boats. He did not know the name of the town. They went ashore and stayed in someone's house.

After a couple of days, they got on another boat and traveled to a seaport. He later found out that the seaport was Hong Kong. This was the island that China ceded to the British Crown in 1842 as the result of the Treaty of Nanking, after the British won the notorious Opium War.[4] The island originated as a fishing village with about 2000 inhabitants plus another 2000 living on boats around the island. Ten years later, the British had developed this small trading post into a strategic seaport.

The woman then sold Ming to a Tanka woman surnamed Cheung. Tankas had been boat dwellers for generations off the coast of South China Sea. As the principal seafaring people of South China, Tankas usually owned large sea-going junks. They engaged in deep-sea fishing or merchandise

---

[4] Concerned over the financial and moral consequences of opium, the Special Commissioner for Southern China, Lin Tse-Hsu, succeeded initially in stemming the opium trade. Britain, however, was not willing to let go of this lucrative trade. In 1842, Britain attacked China, thus starting the "Opium War." China lost the war. The Treaty of Nanking brought the war to a close. As a result, Lin was forced into exile in disgrace. Also, China had to pay for the opium destroyed and consequently ceded Hong Kong Island to the British Crown.

transportation. While they might have immigrated from outside of China, they regarded themselves as Chinese.

Cheung's trade was to buy girls and to ship them to America as prostitutes. Due to the lack of women in San Francisco, trading of women was quite a money-making business. For instance, it was reported that in 1854 a merchant shipped hundreds of girls, each bought for about $50(U.S.) in Canton, and then sold for twenty times that amount in America. Some of those girls were bought, some kidnapped, and some were tricked into going.

Cheung had quite a few men as lovers. Before she left for America, she placed Ming under the custody of one of her men named Fung. Fung had a rather kind heart and even allowed Ming to study in a government school. But Fung's wife was mean. Before Ming could eat every morning and evening, he was required to cook and to do all kinds of chores. If the tasks were not done, she would yell and whip him. Therefore, he was usually very late for school every day. Even though he attended school for about three years, he actually had less than ten months of education. As a result, he could only recognize about fifty words. He thought that he was slow in learning.

Four years later, Cheung returned to Hong Kong to transport more girls to America. This time, she decided to take Ming along.

The boat trip across the Pacific took about two months and was a rough passage. Nevertheless, attracted by opportunities due to the "gold rush" in California, thousands of Chinese still traveled on these boat trips every year. Their search for gold helped coin a popular Chinese name for America, *Gum San*, literally, the "gold mountain." Likewise, San Francisco was named *Kao Gum San* (literally, "the old gold mountain").

The vast ocean was rough. The famous explorer Ferdinand Magellan sailed across it in 1520, and named it "Pacific," meaning "peaceful." Yet, it was not always peaceful. During storms, its waves could toss about even a big ship, and waves could wash over the deck.

Conditions on those ships were also rough. In spite of the efforts of the Hong Kong government to regulate and monitor the transportation, conditions on the ships, especially those carrying Chinese passengers, remained deplorable. Usually, the Chinese were crammed into small quarters in the boat. Many were abused.   The cramped quarters, poor air circulation, poor food and the lack of fresh water resulted in unsanitary conditions. On some of the trips, it was reported that nearly a quarter of the Chinese passengers died. Many of the fortunate ones who arrived at the Golden Gate in San Francisco were weak and sick.

Ming remembered an unusual incident on the voyage. The ship was caught in a storm for three days and three nights. Waves were getting into the ship. Many passengers worried that the ship might break.   Afraid of drowning, they were offering prayers to their gods (Buddha) to plead for protection. As the boat was tossing about on the rough Pacific Ocean, Ming could hardly sleep or sit still.   One night, he suddenly remembered that he had studied about Jesus and the Gospels in a school in Hong Kong. He recalled how Jesus taught His disciples to pray, "Our Father, who art in heaven, hallowed be Thy Name. Thy kingdom come..." So, he prayed the Lord's Prayer. The next day, the sea was calm. He was amazed and treasured the incident in his heart.

CHAPTER 5
San Francisco

After they arrived at San Francisco, Cheung opened a brothel. In those days, girls in these brothels were essentially slaves. They were not paid, and were often mistreated. In Ming's heart, he really hated Cheung's trade and was disgusted by her practice. Yet, he had no other place to live. New to the country, the twelve year old Ming could not do much to change his situation.

After a few months, he was able to make some friends and asked their help to pursue alternatives. He wanted to find any kind of work that would provide room and board. Being desperate to get out, he was willing to accept any pay. At that time, a Chinese live-in house servant earned a starting wage of one and a half dollar a week. Even though room and board was included, the food allowance could be just bread and apple sauce.

He found a job in a Jewish family where he worked for about a year. As for his small earnings, he would give them to Cheung, as a way of repaying her. The new situation was quite a transition from his past. At night, he could even study English in a school set up by the government to help Chinese immigrants. From 6 to 9, every evening, he attended the English class.

At that time, he made a good friend named Ouyang Shing-Chack. Ouyang was a very sincere man and was always willing to help. Like other Buddhists, he believed in reincarnation. As a practicing and devout Buddhist, he had deep respect for any animal life, and was therefore a vegetarian. Even though he was not a Christian, he encouraged Ming to attend the nearby Chinese Church, called *Foke Yam Tong* (literally, "Gospel Hall"). As a result of Ouyang's encouragement, Ming started to attend the Chinese Church every Sunday.

Ming knew of this Chinese Church, as it met in the same building as the English school. Located on Stockton Street, the building[5] served many purposes. The school was on the ground level. The church was right above the school. Pastor Loomis and his family lived on the third floor.

The Chinese church was originally founded in 1853 by Dr. William Speer. Dr. Speer was born in 1822 in New Alexandria, Pennsylvania. After seminary education and ordination, he was commissioned to be a missionary to China in 1846. With his young wife, he arrived in Macau in December 1846. Besides establishing a medical mission, he organized the first Presbyterian Church in Canton, China. His missionary work in China was costly; he lost his wife and infant son due to sickness. In 1850, he returned to America for a furlough to recuperate. After he remarried in 1852, he was commissioned to reach the Chinese in San Francisco. The work of Dr. Speer among the Chinese was ahead of his time in reaching racial minorities. The church that he started was the first Chinese Christian church in America. It was also one of the first Protestant churches in California, for it had been only a few years earlier, in April 1849, that the first Protestant church in California had been organized by Presbyterians in Benicia, twenty miles northeast of San Francisco; and the First Presbyterian Church of San Francisco had been established a month after that.

Dr. Speer faced unusual challenges for his work with the Chinese immigrants. On one hand, they were discriminated against as a despised racial minority. On the other hand, they were exploited by their own people.

The Gold Rush and building of the transcontinental railroad led to immigration of many Chinese, accounting for about a tenth of California's population by 1860. In some of the mining counties, they even constituted almost a third of the

---

[5] The original church building was destroyed during the 1906 Great Earthquake and the related fires.

population. The early welcome of Chinese labor changed to toleration, and then to resentment, and even to discrimination in later years. For instance, there were discriminatory taxes that applied primarily to the Chinese. In 1852, there was the miner's tax of three dollars per month. Then, in 1862, there was the "police tax" on every Chinese male over eighteen who was not paying the miner's tax.

Another example of discrimination occurred in 1854 when Justice Hugh C. Murray of the California Supreme Court persuaded his fellow justices that the provisions in the constitution that excluded the testimonies of Indians and Blacks in cases involving Whites should apply also to the Chinese. Such resentment eventually spread to the U.S. Congress which passed anti-Chinese legislation: the "Naturalization Act" in 1870, which excluded Chinese from citizenship and prohibited the entry of wives of laborers; and the "Chinese Exclusion Act" in 1882, which suspended immigration of Chinese laborers.

Some of the Chinese laborers were also exploited by their own countrymen who served as their creditors. Since many of them came on the boat across the Pacific Ocean through a ticket purchased on credit, they were required to repay their creditors who also became their employers. Because some were paid very low wages, they were subjected to a life-long debt-bondage.

Dr. Speer's missionary work was accompanied by social work. Besides preaching the Christian gospel to the Chinese, Dr. Speer operated a clinic to serve their physical needs. The clinic was much needed since many of the newly arrived Chinese were ill from the unsanitary conditions experienced on the boat trip across the Pacific Ocean. Later, he also obtained signatures to petition the California House and Senate to repeal some of the discriminatory tax laws and succeeded in having them repealed. Thus, he was affectionately called in Chinese "the Friend of Chinese."

In 1857, after pastoring for four years, Dr. Speer became seriously ill and had to return to his home in Pennsylvania to recuperate. Thus, the Chinese Church in San Francisco had no pastor for two years. Many of the original members moved to other places, and some returned to China.

In 1859, Rev. August W. Loomis was appointed by the Presbyterian Board of Foreign Missions in New York to be the pastor of the church. When he took over the church on September 14, 1859, there were only two members left. Prior to assuming this position, Loomis had served as a missionary in China. He first arrived in Macau in 1844. Then, in 1846 to 1849, he served as a missionary in Ningpo, one of the five coastal cities that China was forced to open as a result of the Opium War. He was fluent in the Ningpo dialect. To become more effective in his new position, however, he also learned Cantonese, the common dialect among Chinese in America.

Loomis took advantage of every available means to reach the Chinese. He and his small team of coworkers often went to the piers to greet new immigrants who had just gotten off the boat, passing out tracts and Bibles. This way, they could bring the literature to their places of work, the mines or other little towns. His team often went into homes to explain the gospel. The responses varied. Some people expressed interest, while others flatly rejected his message.

In later years, Loomis also encountered animosity from anti-Chinese groups. For years, he loved and defended the Chinese. As a result, in the 1870's, he was slandered by anti-Chinese cartoons in a racist newspaper published in San Francisco. Nevertheless, his work bore fruit. He was able to reach out to thousands of Chinese. In 1861, he baptized his first Chinese convert. In later years, many more believed.

Loomis had a Chinese assistant, Tsui Shing-Cheung, who became a Christian through the work of the London

Missionary Society[6] in Hong Kong. Ming appreciated Tsui's ministry, for Tsui preached in simple Chinese terms and explained with personal illustrations. Through the simple teaching of the gospel, Ming was convicted of his sins. He understood the nature and consequences of sin.

As he grasped the dreadfulness of sin, Ming deplored even more the immoral work of Cheung. One night, he had a nightmare. He dreamed that people in Cheung's house were dying. The nightmare somehow put him in such a state of awe that he had no peace for several days.

After the nightmare, Ming developed sores under his arm pits. As the sores were very painful, he had difficulty in continuing his work. Therefore, he quit his job and moved in with Tsui to live in the church. Tsui's hospitality deeply touched him.

---

[6] London Missionary Society was the first Protestant group to send missionaries to China. Robert Morrison, the first missionary to China, was sent in 1807 under its auspice.

CHAPTER 6
New Life With A New Name

"Therefore if any man is in Christ, he is a new creature; the old things passed away; behold, new things have come."
                                                    2 Corinthians 5:17

Tsui, the Chinese assistant to the pastor at the church, had a high regard for this young teenager. He knew that Ming had given up a more secure life to have a cleaner environment. Tsui praised him in front of friends and said, "This young man is a noble-minded person. Don't look down on him. We should realize that many great men in history usually have come from a deprived humble background."

Along that line of thought, Tsui gave him a new name, To-Ming (literally, "The Way made clear"). This new name, which he used for the rest of his life, also signified a new beginning in his life.

While living at the church, To-Ming became acquainted with another Christian named Kum-Lam. Kum-Lam treated him well, and even invited him to visit his dwelling where he was employed as a cook. Kum-Lam took the opportunity to explain To-Ming's situation to his boss and his wife. The couple liked To-Ming and allowed him to stay in their home for almost two months.

Kum-Lam's boss, a German doctor, also treated To-Ming's sores. In such a well-cared-for environment, To-Ming's health improved. Every Sunday, Kum-Lam also took To-Ming along to church.

Kum-Lam's boss introduced To-Ming to work in the home of his friends who was a painter of art. Kum-Lam even helped in requesting that the painter's family teach To-Ming English, something that the family was glad to do. Therefore, in the day, he worked around the house, and at night the painter's wife taught him English.

As a result, To-Ming began to understand more English. He also began to wear regular American style clothing, allowing him to travel around the city more freely. Unlike the typical Chinese clothing, the new clothes blended in more with those of other local residents. Also, hoodlums would not harass him anymore.

On Sundays, To-Ming attended church worship, and on Thursday nights, To-Ming would also attend the prayer meeting. His regular attendance and sincerity impressed Pastor Loomis, who gave him a Chinese Bible and a booklet named, "Discussion Between Two Friends." Using a conversation between two friends, the booklet presented the gospel message in simple terms.

The next day, after finishing his chores, and the English lessons, he began to read the booklet. He found, however, that he still could not understand the simple booklet, because of his limited vocabulary. So he prayed that God would open his mind, grant him wisdom, and deliver him from the handicap of illiteracy, and allow him to read the Bible.

"But if any of you lacks wisdom, let him ask of God, who gives to all men generously..." He found the promise in James 1:5 to be real in his life. God answered his prayers. Every Sunday, he listened carefully to Tsui's preaching and tried to learn the words used in the message. After a year of earnest prayers and diligent studies, he noticed great improvement. Now, he could read and write. He was excited that his understanding of language extended beyond the Bible to other books, opening a new horizon in his life.

As he progressed in knowledge and understanding, he grew to appreciate prayer more and more. He began to pray more fervently and frequently. Even while he was working, he learned to pray in his heart. Sometimes, when no one was around, he would even kneel to pray.

A year later, he suddenly felt convicted that he was a sinner. The burden became so great that he could hardly bear it. So, he prayed to Jesus for forgiveness. After that prayer, he experienced a special comfort and peace in his heart.

Having the assurance of faith of the new life in Christ, he asked to be baptized. Pastor Loomis, however, felt that he was too young, and was concerned that he might not know the truth well enough to make a proper decision. Refusing his request, Loomis explained, "If you have a genuine desire to be baptized, delaying a little would not be too late."

One night, after the prayer meeting, To-Ming went to Tsui's room to chat. After he sat down, Tsui asked him, "I have known you for quite some time. I even got a name for you, but I still don't know your surname yet. What is your family name?"

To-Ming was embarrassed and could not answer for a while. After pondering in silence, he said, "Oh, I do not remember. If I recall it, I will let you know." Not wanting to continue the discussion, he left shortly after that reply.

That night, back in his boss's house, he was wondering how he should respond to Tsui's question. Unlike most people, he found that question difficult to answer. As he was kidnaped as a youngster, he could not remember his family name. He said to himself, "I had long forgotten my original family name. What should I do now? What would be a suitable name for me to use?"

As he was pondering, the idea of the Creator as the heavenly Father suddenly dawned on him. He said to himself, "Oh! Jesus is the Creator of heaven and earth. So, in a way, I can say that Jesus is my father. Good! I can follow His name."

The Chinese name for Jesus consisted of two Chinese words, "Ye So" (transliterated from Greek, *Iesous*). Since Chinese surnames were usually monosyllabic, he selected one word. As "So" was a rather common Chinese surname, he chose "So"[7] to be his family name.

The next day, he visited Tsui and told Tsui that his family name was "So." He did not tell Tsui about the origin of his name.

The Chinese culture resembles the old Hebrew culture in emphasizing the meaning of names. Often, names were chosen for a special meaning and purpose. So now, as To-Ming found his new identity in Christ, he had a new full name to go with his new identity. Both his given name and surname reflected his new identity and direction in life.

The following year, he again requested baptism. Recognizing To-Ming's maturity and understanding of the gospel, Pastor Loomis consented. The name used at baptism was "So To-Ming." Thus, he was baptized at the age of sixteen, in approximately 1861.

Seeing that To-Ming had confessed his faith in Christ, and had been baptized, Ouyang gave up his Buddhist practices. Ouyang was so moved by the reality of the new faith in Ming's life that he too wanted to become a Christian. Because of their newly found common faith, To-Ming and Ouyang became very close friends, almost like brothers. Their faith also grew together. Some years later, Ouyang even became a preacher and pastored the branch church in Sacramento.

Having acquired a new surname did not mean that To-Ming had no desire to know his original family name. After he became a Christian, he knelt down every day and prayed to God that he could find his place of origin and see his mother.

From time to time, thoughts about Cheung still bothered him. He detested her immoral trade and livelihood. He wanted to cut off all ties. Yet, he was also troubled because

---

[7] The same word is pronounced "Su" in Mandarin. To conform to the standard Chinese surname, the writing of the Chinese character, "So," was also modified, i.e. the "flower" radical was added to the top of the Chinese character.

she had paid a price to purchase him from his kidnapper. Also, she had provided his sustenance for quite a few years.

Thinking about the life of Moses in the Bible gave him insight on how to deal with his dilemma. He thought about how Moses had been reared by the Egyptian princess for many years. She had even put him through the palace court education in Egypt. In a sense, Moses should have been grateful for her care. Yet later, he had left her, cut all ties, and followed God gladly.

To-Ming compared his own experience with that of Moses. Even though Cheung had provided for him for a few years, the treatment was nothing compared to what Moses had received. Furthermore, her immoral trade was deplorable. Therefore, To-Ming decided to sever all ties with Cheung, and did not contact her any more. From that time onward, his attention was focused on studying English.

CHAPTER 7
Return With A Mission

"Therefore, we are ambassadors for Christ..."

2 Corinthians 5:20

To-Ming continued to work in the painter's house for about three years. He realized that working most of the day left little time for him to study English. So, he decided to quit his job so he could spend more time studying English. The painter's wife had tears in her eyes when he departed. She was sad to see him go.

He wanted to find a job that would allow more time to study English. Seeing his determination to learn, Pastor Loomis decided to teach him English half a day and let him work half a day. To-Ming sometimes studied until one or two in the morning before he slept.

Since To-Ming had not visited Cheung for almost three years, Cheung had not received any payment from him. Anxious for the money she used to receive, she sent underlings to collect money from To-Ming. Wanting to cut all ties, he refused. Not giving up easily, she requested a policeman to visit To-Ming, as a way to pressure him.

When the policeman showed up at the door of the church, he informed To-Ming of Cheung's request for money. To-Ming immediately informed Pastor Loomis. Loomis became very angry, and rebuked the policeman, telling him that laws in America did not allow for that kind of bondage and financial arrangement. Loomis also mentioned that he might file charges against the policeman. The stern warning took care of the problem. The policeman left and never returned. Cheung did not send any more messengers. Even when her underlings met To-Ming in the street, they did not bother him.

Because of To-Ming's hard work and diligent study, his body weakened. Quite often, he was sick. Loomis was concerned that his health might be ruined before finishing his study. One day, Loomis called for To-Ming and said, "In the near future, Dr. Kerr, a medical doctor in our denomination, will be returning to China as a missionary. He will be passing by here. He and his wife will be staying with me. I want to recommend you to him to be his apprentice. Learning medicine has many benefits. Besides gaining insights on how to take care of your own body, you can help other people suffering from sicknesses. Learning medicine will be much better than learning English. For, if you were to succeed in learning English, you will be the primary benefactor. If you learn medicine, however, others will also benefit from your effort. Wouldn't that be a much better vocational choice?"

To-Ming replied, "Your advice is very good indeed. If Dr. Kerr would not mind taking me, I will be glad to go."

As Pastor Loomis recommended, Dr. and Mrs. Kerr interviewed To-Ming. They were pleased with To-Ming's faith and persistence to learn. Besides agreeing to take him to China as his student, Dr. Kerr even promised to pay his room and board expenses.

To-Ming was very fortunate to have Dr. John Glasgow Kerr as a teacher. Dr. Kerr was one of the most well-known missionary doctors in Southern China. He started his medical missionary career in Canton in 1854, staying there until 1901. He managed the Canton Christian Hospital. He had trained many medical doctors and published quite a few textbooks on medicine. In addition, he started the first leprosy sanitarium in China.

While getting ready for the trip, To-Ming was concerned about his shortage of money. After working so hard for seven years, he had saved about a hundred and thirty dollars. Since Tsui had borrowed a hundred dollars, he had only thirty some dollars left. In need of money, To-Ming sought Tsui to clear the debt. Tsui could not repay him then, but he did promise that he would return the money as soon as he earned enough.

Yet Tsui's promise did not solve To-Ming's immediate financial need.

To-Ming said to himself, "If I spend all my savings on the ticket, I will not have any money left to buy another set of clothes after I get to Canton."

One day, Lee Kum-Lun, a classmate in his English class, came to visit To-Ming. After operating a successful business, he was returning to China. Lee said, "I am returning to China this month. I heard that you are also going back on the same boat. I am really glad, because I will have a companion on this long trip."

To-Ming explained his desire of going back to China to study medicine. On finding out that he did not have enough money, Lee said, "Don't worry about money. The boat ticket is forty dollars. I will pay for you. In the future, if you have money, you can pay me back."

Lee's love and generosity deeply touched To-Ming. He noted in his journal that this incident was another of God's special provisions in time of need.

The day came for To-Ming's departure for China. His friends and Pastor Loomis gave him gifts and bid him farewell. Their love deeply moved To-Ming. Not having any other earthly relatives, these people were his family. Reflecting on the kindness of Pastor Loomis in being his teacher and mentor, his eyes were filled with tears as he shook hands to bid farewell.

Thus, in 1867, at the age of 21, To-Ming left San Francisco to travel with Dr. Kerr to Canton to start his medical training.

CHAPTER 8
Marriage Arranged

Back in China, the land of his birth, To-Ming's life took on a new dimension. He was starting a new career path in a new city.

Since he had never lived in Canton before, the city was also new for him. Quite a contrast from the surrounding areas, Canton was the largest city in Southern China. For centuries, this was the only seaport in China open to the outside world. Canton was also the capital of the province where most of the overseas Chinese came from. Their movements back and forth made this city more open to new ideas. Furthermore, the city was only a hundred miles from Hong Kong. For these reasons, missionaries naturally found this city an ideal place to start their work.

The Canton Hospital stood out as an excellent example of the achievements of the Christian missionaries. It was founded in 1835, by Dr. Peter Parker, the first missionary doctor to China. It was the first Western medical hospital in China. Dr. Kerr had expanded the work since he had become in charge of the missionary hospital in 1855. The related medical college, founded in 1866, was also the first medical school in China. It was built next to the First Presbyterian Church. Being the first hospital, it was named just "Canton Hospital" in English. In Chinese, however, the hospital was known as "Pok-Chee," literally, "helping many." This was also the first institution teaching Western medicine in China.[8] Along with other

---

[8] Dr. Sun Yat-Sen, the founder of the Republic of China (1912), also started his medical training in this medical college in 1886. Later, it combined with Ling-Nang University, a Christian university where Dr. Happer was the president from 1887 to 1891. In the early days of the People's Republic of China (1950), it was named South

hospitals founded by missionaries in China, they offered significant contributions to health care in China.

In Canton Hospital, To-Ming studied medicine under Dr. Kerr. As he had decided to pursue this new career, he studied hard. In addition, he set aside time to study Chinese. Even though it sounded strange, he needed to learn Chinese so he could serve his own people, the Chinese. Chinese proficiency was necessary because he had been taken to America at an early age, and did not have the benefit of a normal Chinese education.

After a year in Canton, Mrs. Tseng, an older lady at the church, came to know To-Ming well. Because of her age and her concern for the welfare of others, she was affectionately nicknamed "Tseng San-Sum" (literally, the third aunt in the Tseng family). She posed an unusual question to him, "Brother To-Ming, are you married?"

To-Ming replied, "I came back from *Gum San*, but I don't have a lot of *Gum* (literally—"I came back from the Gold Mountain but I don't have a lot of gold"). It is only because of Dr. Kerr's kindness that I can study medicine. So, I am determined to put my time and energy into studying medicine. I dare not think about marriage now."

Aunt Tseng then explained, "Let me tell you why I am talking about personal matters like this. I know a girl from the family of Pong. She was Mrs. Happer's student for several years. She is a Christian already. Yet, a few years ago, after the death of Mrs. Happer, Rev. Happer returned to America. As a result, her parents took her back to their home. I just found out that her family recently moved to Hong Kong. I am afraid that she may end up marrying a non-Christian. That is why I came. I am not a match-maker."

Dr. Andrew Patton Happer was well respected by Christians in Canton. He was the first American Presbyterian

---

China Medical College. In 1985, it was renamed Sun Yat-Sen University of Medical Sciences.

missionary doctor to serve in Canton in 1844. Dr. Speer
worked with him for a few years when he served in Canton in
1846. In addition to operating a clinic, he opened a school for
boys in 1850. From 1851 to 1853, the Happers opened a
boarding school for girls, the first one in China.

Having great respect for the Happers and Aunt Tseng, To-
Ming consented, "I would consider marrying her if her parents
don't mind my being poor, and are willing to wait until I finish
my medical studies. When I become independent, then we can
talk about marriage. If I do not have to rush into getting
married, I think that marriage may not be a bad idea."

With that conditional consent, Aunt Tseng went to Hong
Kong to talk with Miss Pong's parents. Learning that To-Ming
was still not financially independent, her parents were hesitant.

When Mr. Lai Man-San, Dr. Andrew Happer's private
Chinese tutor, heard about this, he wrote Miss Pong's father
immediately. Amazingly, Lai's letter of recommendation was
effective. Her father changed his mind. He requested that To-
Ming send a betrothal present as soon as possible.[9]

While pleased with the positive response, he was surprised
at the early request for the betrothal present. To-Ming did not
know what to do because he did not have the money for the
betrothal present. He became quite depressed. He described
his dilemma with a typical Chinese idiom: "To advance or to
retreat is equally difficult."

About this time, Chou Chi-Ming, To-Ming's friend from
San Francisco, returned to China. He was passing through
Canton on his way back to his own village to see his mother.
Still carrying his unpacked suitcases, Chou dropped by to see
him. Since they had not seen each other for two years, they
talked for a long time that night. To-Ming shared his desire to
become betrothed.

---

[9] The betrothal present was an Oriental custom. It was like
today's engagement ring, to show that the couple was serious.

Chou said, "Don't worry, I have money in my suitcase. Pay me back only if you have money in the future." Chou took out forty dollars for To-Ming to prepare his betrothal present. To-Ming knew again in his heart that God was providing at the right moment.

After his engagement, To-Ming concentrated especially hard on studying medicine. Three years later, after an examination by both Dr. Kerr and Dr. Wong Fan, he was granted the position of Assistant Doctor at the Canton Hospital.[10]

After To-Ming had finished his medical training, Aunt Tseng came to urge him to get married. "Dr. So To-Ming, Congratulations! I guess that you can get married now. Am I correct?"

"I thought that we had agreed earlier that I will not get married until I have enough money. Look, even though I have finished my training, I still have no money. How can I get married?" To-Ming protested.

Tseng replied, "You are absolutely right. However, Miss Pong wrote me a few times saying that her mother had been sick for some time. She is concerned that her mother may not be alive much longer. Her mother's desire is that she can see her daughter married while she is still alive. Miss Pong just wants to fulfill her mother's wish."

To-Ming still would not consent. At the end of that year, Dr. Happer returned to Canton from America. Tseng told Happer that his student, Miss Pong, was betrothed to To-Ming. Happer was very happy and said, "She is a pleasant girl. My wife loved her very much. She was quiet and polite, quite different from other girls around her. After I returned to America after my wife's death, I have been concerned that she

---

[10] Dr. Wong Fan was the first medical doctor trained by the missionaries. After being sent to study in the medical school in the University of Edinburgh, he returned to serve in the Canton Hospital.

might be married to a non-Christian. Now that she is engaged to To-Ming, I am very pleased."

Dr. Happer continued, "You know, they really match each other. I have heard a lot of good things about To-Ming from his former church in San Francisco. His friends praised and respected him. They all knew him well."

Aunt Tseng said, "But, he does not want to get married yet. I really don't know what to do."

Dr. Happer said, "Why don't you tell him to come and see me?"

After being invited, To-Ming visited Dr. Happer who urged him to get married soon. To-Ming explained, "But I don't have enough money to provide for a family yet. How can I proceed?"

Happer then said, "Try your best to come up with some money. If you still don't have enough, Dr. Kerr and I will lend you some money. You can pay us back from your salary in monthly installments."

With that kind of support, To-Ming had nothing more to say. He knew that he should proceed.

To come up with more money, To-Ming wrote to Tsui in America for the money owed him. When his other friends in America heard about his situation, they were more than eager to help. They even sent an additional thirty some dollars as a wedding gift. To-Ming was surprised to receive the additional amount.

The Pong family requested To-Ming to go to Hong Kong to meet the bride. At this time, his good old friend, Ouyang Shing-Chack, came back from America. Ouyang accompanied To-Ming to Hong Kong and was his only close friend at the wedding. Having no relatives at all, Ouyang's presence meant much to To-Ming.

The wedding was held at an Anglican Church. Rev. Dana led the prayer. Those who attended the banquet were primarily from that church.

The day after the wedding, To-Ming returned to Canton with his bride. When the boat pulled up to the pier in the afternoon, the new couple was surprised to be greeted by a group of friends waiting to take care of their luggage. Then, To-Ming saw Dr. Happer's family and the other pastors from the church. They had been waiting for some time. They invited the new couple to Dr. Kerr's home for a time of prayer.

Entering the house, To-Ming was surprised to see the room filled with his friends. They were formally dressed for the occasion. After prayer, Dr. Kerr sent people to tell the restaurant to get the food ready. Having known the time of their arrival, Dr. Kerr had prepared the surprise reception party ahead of time. To-Ming was thankful to God and expressed his gratitude for Dr. Kerr's kindness and generosity. To add to the celebration, Kerr had ordered a Chinese banquet for To-Ming and his friends. They sat around tables to enjoy the food and the fellowship.

More than thirty people, including Chinese and Westerners, attended the banquet at Dr. Kerr's home that night. To-Ming was grateful for the love of Dr. Kerr and Rev. Happer. Again, he noted that it was the grace of God that enabled him to receive these showers of blessings.

Some years later, To-Ming reflected on this joyous occasion, and noted how the sequence of events had unfolded one by one. He was amazed how God used different types of people at different locations to bless him. He noted that he first received the seed of the gospel during his brief attendance in a school in Hong Kong. Then, he came to understand the gospel fully and was baptized in the Presbyterian Church in America. Finally at his wedding, an Anglican pastor conducted the ceremony, which was followed with prayer by an American Presbyterian pastor.

CHAPTER 9
Looking For His Original Home

Besides enjoying success in his medical career, To-Ming was blessed with a Christian home with quite a few children: four sons and three daughters. He was grateful for God's blessings. Nevertheless, his desire to find his original home remained strong. He continued to pray earnestly that God might lead him back home.

After his return to China, one of his best friends was Leung Chu-Sun, a member of his church. Even though they had known each other for more than ten years, To-Ming never revealed his background to him.

One day, To-Ming met Chu-Sun's older brother, Yee-Fung. Somehow, Yee-Fung's countenance left an unforgettable impression. Unlike his younger brother who was more acculturated to Canton, Yee-Fung still had a slight accent. To-Ming said to himself, "Yee-Fung's accent and appearance remind me of folks from the village where I came from. Someday, I must talk to him. Maybe he can tell me what his village looks like. Then I can see whether it matches what I remember about my own village." Yet for some time, To-Ming could not find any opportunity to talk to him.

One day, Yee-Fung dropped by To-Ming's house to chat. Remembering his desire to find out about his own background, To-Ming asked, "Brother Yee-Fung, I was lost as a small child during the famine, about the time of the Taiping Rebellion. This was probably during the early years of Hsien-Feng's reign as the Ching Emperor.[11] I have forgotten the name of my village. I even forgot my family's surname. One of the few names that I can still remember is that of my maternal

---

[11] 1851-1861

grandmother's village, which was called Yiu-Koo. The neighboring village was called Law-Chu."

"Well, I know of two places that have the name of Yiu-Koo. One is near Kim-Lee and the other is near Sun-Kiu. I am from the one near Kim-Lee. I wonder which is the one your grandmother belonged to? Why don't you tell me a little more about her village? Just tell me whatever you remember. I'll see whether the descriptions match mine."

To-Ming searched his memory and gave a detailed account, "My village was very close to a town. If I wanted to go to my grandma's home, I had to pass through the town. Then I would go on the dike by the side of the town. There was a large temple near the middle of the dike. That dike led directly to her village. The distance was about four or five *li*.[12] In front of the village was a ridge full of pine trees. Around that ridge was a wooden gate. Then, there were two ponds with a small dike, about two or three feet wide. Walking another 100 steps would take me to her home."

"From what you described, we may be from the same village. On my next trip home, I want you to come with me to my humble village for a tour. Then you will get to see for yourself whether my village is yours too."

"I am very grateful for your invitation!"

After Yee-Fung went home, he told his brother, "I talked with To-Ming today. I think that we may be from the same area originally."

A few months passed after that encounter. One night, about 10 P.M., Chu-Sun unexpectedly dropped by To-Ming's residence. Surprised at such a late visit, To-Ming rushed to the door to greet his best friend, "Welcome! Coming at such a late hour, I trust that you have some good news for me."

Chu-Sun said, "Dr. So, I am coming to invite you to come with us for a tour of my home town. I hope that you can bring some medicine with you. We can kill two birds with one stone.

---

[12] about two miles

On one hand, you can treat some poor, sick, people in the village. Also, you can see for yourself whether my village is the same as your maternal grandmother's."

"That is very kind of you to invite me."

"I have also invited Mr. Ou Fung-Chee to go with you. I have already paid for the fares. I will be leaving for my home village tomorrow and I will prepare all the necessary arrangements for you in the village. A couple of days later, my brother will accompany both of you on the trip."

"I am deeply grateful for your brotherly love."

"Don't say things like that. We are brothers-in-Christ. We even belong to the same local church."

The next day, To-Ming went to Canton Hospital to request leave for a few days. When his medical students found out where he was going, they gave him a very interesting explanation for Mr. Leung's invitation. They told him, "Mr. Leung has gone back to his village to conduct the wedding for his son. That is a happy occasion. He probably wants to invite you to his son's wedding and to attend the banquet."

To-Ming was glad to find out the special occasion of the Leung family. He hurried home immediately to prepare a wedding gift.

CHAPTER 10
Finding His Original Family Name

Two days later, To-Ming started his trip from Canton. The day was the 19th of the 11th month in the 8th year when Kuang-Hsu was the emperor.[13]

While arranging for people to take care of his luggage, his nose began bleeding. Since he was afraid that the bleeding would not stop, he felt that he should cancel the trip.

Knowing that To-Ming had been thinking about the trip for the past two days, his wife urged him, "Come on! This trip may be an excellent opportunity to find your mother. If you don't go now, you may never have another opportunity."

Words like that motivated and encouraged To-Ming. He decided to proceed. Bidding farewell to his wife, he said, "Take care of yourself. Pray without ceasing, and wait for good news."

The agreed-upon meeting point was at the Sandy Bar Gospel Church, near the Pearl River. When To-Ming arrived there, Ou Fung-Chee and Leung Yee-Fung were waiting there already. Soon, they got on a boat. About noon, sails were set and the boat was on its way.

The direct distance was about thirty miles. Boating distance through the Pearl River delta was normally about fifty miles. During the winter, however, the water level of the Pearl River was lower, and the boat had to take routes with deeper water. Therefore, the boat had to go by Fu-San, a large and prominent town on the Pearl River delta. With the longer route, To-Ming could see more of the countryside. There were many villages intermingled with lush woods along the river banks. The boat also passed by many brick kilns. Having lived

---

[13] The Ching Dynasty regnal calendar was based on lunar calendar. The equivalent time should be about late December 1881 or early January 1882.

in cities most of the time since his abduction out of his own village, he was attracted by the pretty scenery.

In the evening, the owner of the boat joined them for dinner. The owner also came from the same district as Yee-Fung. From the clothing and behavior of Ou and To-Ming, the owner knew that they were not from the area. The owner whispered to Yee-Fung and inquired about the purpose of their trip. After hearing that To-Ming was visiting his home village, the owner and his crew just stared at To-Ming.

The next morning, they arrived at Sam-Shui (literally, "three rivers"). The place was so named because the town was situated at the confluence of three tributaries of the Pearl River. Before proceeding, the boat had to stop for an inspection by the custom officer. The custom office was set up at this strategic location by the provincial government for inspecting goods and collecting taxes.

After making a few stops, Yee-Fung pointed his finger ahead and said, "The hill ahead of us is called the "Horse's Mouth." After that, we will arrive at Kim-Lee, the town near my village."

They arrived at Kim-Lee at about 11 A.M. Chu-Sun's son-in-law, Wong Wen, was waiting at the pier. Yee-Fung took care of the luggage and called for a boat to take the luggage to his home through a small stream.

Wong Wen guided them to his house. As To-Ming walked through the dike, he looked around and recognized a couple of places. The closer he got to Wong's house, the more places he could recognize.

When Wong's father got news of their arrival, he came out to welcome them. He also told his family to prepare breakfast for the guests. (The typical Cantonese in those days ate their first meal around 11 A.M.)

A little while later, Yee-Fung arrived with the luggage. Yee-Fung said, "Dr. So, after we finish eating, I will walk with you into town. Let's see whether you can recognize the place. Then we will go to Yiu-Koo village."

To-Ming answered, "That's great!"

Dishes of gourmet food were set on the dinner table. Having such a good meal for the first day of visit really touched To-Ming. He expressed his heartfelt gratitude to Yee-Fung for his kindness and hospitality.

After the meal, Yee-Fung took To-Ming to tour the town. The marketplace was just across the stream from Mr. Wong's bookstore. The stream was about a hundred feet wide. This was the stream where the boat carrying the luggage came through.

Ou Fung-Chee, Wong Wen, Wong Chi-Yu, Leung Yee-Fung, and To-Ming walked through the town together. They saw a big temple. The court yard in front of the temple was a busy place. Many hawkers were selling things from their baskets. By this time, To-Ming could recognize the place quite well. So he said to Yee-Fung, "How do you go to the next village?"

"Just go through that lane by the side of the temple."

As they walked down that lane, called the Righteous Lane, To-Ming saw a few rice stores. Scenes of his childhood started to come to his mind. He remembered that he used to walk down that same lane, passing by those rice stores, begging for food.

He also passed by the place where he, as a young beggar, had a stomach cramp. He recalled how he had been lying on his side shivering in the cold rain. He could always remember this spot because that was where the kind merchant had shown compassion and had given him money.

Looking down the mound, he saw two dragon boats. These dragon boats were used for sculling competitions during the festival on the fifth day of the fifth month in the lunar calendar. The festival was meant to commemorate Chu-Yuen, a faithful Chinese official (300 B.C.). The dragon boats sat by the river bank, just like thirty years ago, during To-Ming's childhood.

Excitedly, To-Ming announced to his friends, "That is my village right across the bridge."

"That is Mu Sun Lee village. Most people there belong to the TO[14] family." The two Wongs and Yee-Fung, the three natives, exclaimed together.

Wong Chi-Yu had to leave early to take care of his business. So the four men continued their walk to the hill. They passed by a small temple. To-Ming remembered this building well because he had used this temple as a rain shelter or rest stop. The temple, however, seemed to be located at a different place. So he asked Yee-Fung about the change in location.

"You are absolutely correct. The villagers moved it because of *feng shui*.[15] The move happened only two or three years ago."

"*Feng shui*" had been a prevalent philosophy of placement in China. The influence in rural areas was especially pronounced. Literally, it means "wind" and "water." *Feng Shui* was based on superstition, believing that forces exist in every locality to influence the living and descendants of the dead. Concerned relatives sometimes would hire *feng shui*

---

[14] This surname "TO" is a different word from the "To" in "To-Ming". However, both words has the same pronunciation in Cantonese.

[15] *Feng Shui* is also called geomancy. Besides the belief in the cosmic influence of placement, it has the appearance of an art of stable design. The philosophy was quite influential in the Orient, especially in rural China. (Like many of the other Eastern religions, this one is becoming more popular even in the Western world.) Due to concern for the most favorable influences, heights and shapes of buildings may be modified, and sites of constructions, even dams, may be relocated. In places where buildings cannot be moved, mirrors, often in octagon shapes, were used to counteract unfavorable influences or unstable conditions.

consultants to select grave sites to find the most beneficial influences on descendants. In like manner, *feng shui* would be taken into account for construction of buildings. Existing buildings were sometimes moved if there was enough concern about unfavorable influences. In this case, to seek improvement on their fate, the villagers had taken great pain and effort to relocate the temple.

After they crossed the bridge, To-Ming walked ahead of all his friends. Now that he could recognize the place, he felt like changing roles. Instead of being a visitor to the village, he could become the guide. As he walked towards the village and looked across the farms, scenes from his childhood raced through his mind.

As To-Ming surveyed the neighborhood, he found the old house where he used to live. He began to weep. He never thought that he could ever come back to this house after thirty some years. Trying to hide his emotion, he wiped away his tears. He sighed and thanked God in his heart, "Thank you Lord, for Your wonderful mercy and matchless grace."

Walking through the village, he saw a hill with a few huge trees. As a child, he used to play and bathe under the shade of these trees. The trees and the scenery had not changed much in almost thirty years. For him, it was like stepping into a time machine and going back thirty years.

As he walked past the path by the hill, he remembered that this was the place where his uncle had met him on his way to Po-Po's village. He remembered the scene when his uncle had struck him to the ground after finding out that he wanted to go to Po-Po's home. He started to think about how he used to live alone as a child, how his uncle and aunt had not treated him like their nephew. Memories of the suffering from hunger and cold weather as a child overwhelmed him. He wanted to share his feeling with Ou. He was, however, so filled with emotion that he could not speak much to any of his friends.

Looking up, he saw the mound where his father and grandparents were buried. He was so taken aback that he just stood, dumb-founded, for a while. Since the place was overgrown with bushes, he could not tell which one was his father's tomb.

Later, he led his friends down to the ancestral hall. The hall was the place where the clan put up name plates of their ancestors to pay respect. As was the case with ancestral halls throughout Southern China, this building was a center of activity for the village. Besides providing a social hall for the clan, the building might serve as a school for the children.

The building looked exactly the same, except that the tree in the front yard was gone. More houses had been built around it. Looking up at the marble slab lintel above the door, he saw five big Chinese characters, which meant "The TO Family Ancestral Hall". It was at this moment that he realized that his real family name was "TO."

As they were milling around the ancestral hall, his friends were perplexed that the name plate on the ancestral hall did not match his surname. They wondered why his surname was "SO" and not "TO."

CHAPTER 11
Finding His Old House

After spending some time at the TO Ancestral Hall, To-Ming and his friends continued their walk, passing by the Lee Family Ancestral Hall. In such a countryside, it was easy for the local residents to spot visitors. In rural areas, residents usually knew almost everybody else. In addition, a group of city dwellers who talked and dressed a little differently from the local residents would always attract attention. Quite a few villagers were standing outside gazing at this group of strangers, thinking that they were *feng shui* consultants surveying the area.

To-Ming recognized the small lane by his old house. He walked quickly down the lane. He found his old house still intact. He remembered that his father used to hold him and sit in front of this door. He then recalled how he used to live all by himself, begging in the day time, cooking for himself, and using rags and hay as covering against the cold.

Scenes from his miserable childhood raced through his mind. He sighed deeply as he paced the area. Oblivious to the rugged path with uneven stones, he stepped on the wrong place and almost fell.

Then, they walked by his uncle's house. Unlike the other section, this neighborhood had seen much change. Quite a few new houses had been built nearby.

They saw an old woman, about 70 years old, entering the little house at the foot of the hill. Too emotional, To-Ming motioned Ou to inquire for him.

Stepping forward, Ou asked, "Lady, may I ask you a question? About 30 years ago, during the Taiping Rebellion, a child was lost from here. Now he is coming back to visit. Do you know whether his uncle is still alive?"

"I have not heard of any cases like that in my family. I am from the Chow family. Furthermore, that was too long ago, and too many things have happened since then. I can't remember that far back. You may get more detailed information from some of the men standing around there."

Walking further, To-Ming and his friends met a few men who invited them to the ancestral hall to talk more. A few people in the hall began to discuss among themselves who this lost child could be. Then one person spoke up, "Don't tell me that he is Elder Kwong-Tai's grandson, TO Pei-Chin's son."

Those names did not mean much to To-Ming. Even though he found out later that these names were indeed his ancestors' names, he had never heard them mentioned before. When he was young, nobody had told him his parents' names. There had been no need to know, as children never addressed their parents by their names due to respect.

After a little while, several people started to gather around to find out what was happening. There were about thirty to forty people milling around. Among them, an elderly woman recognized To-Ming's face. She came forward and made an unusual claim.

"Tseng-Po!" The woman called To-Ming by his childhood nick-name and exclaimed, "It's got to be you. Your silhouette hasn't changed much. You are just taller and fairer. I am your second paternal aunt, wife of your second paternal uncle, Kung-Chin."

Ou immediately asked, "Where is his mother? Do you happen to know her whereabouts?"

She replied, "His parents died long time ago."

Ou said, "He already knows that his father died when he was young, but he remembers that his mother was still living. Please tell us whether she is still living."

"His mother left a long time ago," the women replied.

"Well, he remembers clearly that his mother was still alive when he was a small child. Now, after years of hardship, he has come all the way back here to find his village and family.

He went through all these years because he still wants to see the face of his mother. If you do not know clearly whether she is still alive or not, please don't speak rashly to disturb his heart," Ou again spoke on To-Ming's behalf.

The woman then admitted quietly, "It's true that his mother did not die when he was still young. She remarried and moved to another village called Bamboo Island. Most of the people in that village belong to the Eng family."

After hearing about Bamboo Island Village, Yee-Fung said, "We can help you find Bamboo Island Village. Actually, my daughter-in-law came from the Bamboo Island Village. She used to live right next to the Eng family."

While they were talking, Ting, a distant cousin from the TO family volunteered to take To-Ming around. He guided To-Ming to his old house, his uncle's house, and his grandfather's house. Pointing at To-Ming's old house, Ting said, "Your uncle Hon-Chin died without leaving much money to even take care of the funeral. So your house was sold to my older brother. And your uncle's house was sold to my father Long-Chin." [16]

By then many more of his relatives had come out and were calling him by his childhood nickname. He was so moved by what was happening that he could not speak anymore. So he urged Ou and Leung to leave. But the people still surrounded Ou and Leung and told them more about his childhood. They also inquired about the intervening years of To-Ming.

When To-Ming heard their discussion of his childhood, he could contain himself no longer, so he just dragged Wong down

---

[16] The Chinese often uses generation names, i.e., paternal cousins share the first or second word of the given names. Sometimes, even third and fourth cousins may have the same generation names. Thus, it is quite easy to recognize relatives from the same clan, as they have the same family name and generation name. In some families, female cousins may follow a generation name that is different from the male cousins.

the slope to the side of the pond to wait for his other companions to leave. Nevertheless, looking at the pond also evoked old memories of events during the Taiping Rebellion. This pond was where his cousins had saved him by grabbing him into a boat and rowing to the middle of the pond.

He took another deep breath. It seemed that everything around the village evoked painful memories of the past. Looking back at the growing crowd gathering, the whole village appeared to be shaken by the incident.

To-Ming found out that many people in this clan knew his companions. Ting's wife addressed Yee-Fung's with the proper given name. Quite a few of the other women gathering around also knew Wong's name. It turned out that Ting's wife was married to Leung's relatives. After finding out that they were relatives, they continued to talk longer. Traditional Chinese, especially those who live in the country side, like to extend special courtesy to relatives. Besides addressing relatives by proper titles, they exchange news about each other's family, sometimes even offer gifts.

Finally, Ou and Yee-Fung came to join To-Ming. Ting walked with them for some distance to see them off. Seeing that Ting's eyes were wet with tears, Ou commented, "His face does resemble yours. He seems to have a love for you. I believe that he is really closely related to you."

On their way back, they met To-Ming's paternal aunt. She had walked the long distance to tell To-Ming that his mother was originally from the Yiu-Koo Village, where most people were surnamed Tong.

After thanking her, To-Ming and his friends walked back to the Wong's residence. He went to Wong's study so he could write home immediately, knowing that his wife and children would share his joy. He was, however, so filled with emotion, that he could not write legibly. So he asked Ou to write for him.

The letter was addressed to Ying-Fun, his eldest son. The letter was as follows:

Nov. 20, 9th hour (4 P.M.)

To my dear son, Ying-Fun,[17]

Since I left home on the 19th, I was blessed every step of the way. We arrived at the town of Kim-Lee safely. On the 20th, along with Mr. Leung Yee-Fung, Mr. Ou Fung-Chee, we went to Mu-Sun-Lee village. In that village, I found my old clan. Thank God for His guidance, I even found the house where I used to live as a child. I met a paternal aunt, and a cousin who are still living in that house. Quite a few elderly people even remember me and called me by my childhood nickname. Some of them still recognized my face.

I recognized all the little paths very well. I even recognized the places where I used to play as a child. It was like going back to the scenes in my memory.

Today, my desire to find my original home, cherished for so many years, is finally fulfilled. I really thank God for His rich blessing. Our family should all thank God together.

Furthermore, I heard that my own mother is still alive, and is living in Bamboo Island Village. Tomorrow, I will go and find her. When I have more good news, I will let you know as soon as possible.

Please tell Mother all these events, so that she can rejoice with me. Continue to pray earnestly day and

---

[17] Even though he was the second child, he was the oldest son, and had the primary responsibility to care for the family. This may be the reason why To-Ming addressed the letter to him, rather than to his older sister or mother. He also became a medical doctor. Later, he practiced medicine in Hong Kong, and was known as Dr. Coxion To. A very kind man, he often extended medical help to relatives that were not as well off. In his old age, he attended the same Methodist church as the author.

night. Attend to the door and my affairs. If any patients come to see me about medical problems, please tell them that I will be back on the 25th. Take care.

Father

CHAPTER 12
Tour of Po-Po's Village

After chatting for a short time at the Wong's residence, Leung Yee-Fung suggested, "It will be getting dark soon. Why don't we go to visit Yiu-Koo Village? Tomorrow, I will take you for a tour of the village to find your maternal uncle's house. I have already asked someone to go to Bamboo Island Village to fetch your mother, to invite her to come for reunion."

To-Ming was moved by Yee-Fung's consideration and love.

To-Ming set out again with Yee-Fung and Ou. The three men passed over the dike. The path was still the same as during his childhood. After a mile, they saw a big temple. The temple, located between the village and the town, served as an ideal location for tired villagers walking on this path to take breaks.

In front of the temple stood a big old tree, with a trunk of about fifteen feet in circumference. It was at least a hundred years old. He remembered that he used to pass by this tree on his way to his Po-Po's house, usually carried on the back by his maternal uncle. During heavy rains, they would take shelter in this temple. In the hot summer days, they sometimes would rest under the shade of this old tree.

"I wonder when this temple was built? Which dynasty would that be?" To-Ming asked.

"This temple was rebuilt only a few years ago," Yee-Fung replied.

Passing by the temple, he saw the Yiu-Koo Hill, which was thriving with pine trees. To-Ming was very happy because he knew that his Po-Po's house was near. He quickened his pace. Near the village entrance, he saw an old kapok tree (wood cotton tree), just like years ago. The tree was several arm lengths around, planted near the foot of the dike. He remembered that during the harvest time, his maternal uncle used to eat lunch under this tree.

About a few hundred feet away, on the side of the dike, were a few threshing floors. He remembered how he used to help his maternal uncle thresh and dry grain. He recalled the kindness and the care of his uncle. It was only after his uncle's execution for false charges during the Taiping Rebellion that To-Ming had to go through a tough life. He thought of his time of wandering, not even knowing where he had come from. Thirty years had passed; he knew that his grandmother must have died. Those thoughts brought tears again to his eyes.

At the village entrance, he saw a temple named Kwong-Wei (literally, "light-mercy"), built at the foot of the pine hill. He remembered the time when he had a very bad cough when he was young. Since he did not get well after a long time, his maternal uncle had carried him here to ask the monk for medicine.

To-Ming remembered that this temple had been a quiet and well-kept place. There used to be pots of flowers neatly lining the entrance. It was indeed a good place for a retreat.

Now, the building was vacant. The place was desolate and even the stone steps were overgrown with weeds. Noting the contrast of the present scene with his memory, To-Ming inquired, "This temple used to be a quiet and well-kept place. How come it is in such bad shape? This place used to have a monk who helped to cure people. Is he still around?"

"The monk died a long time ago." Yee-Fung replied. "One of the monk's disciples filled the position. The new monk didn't uphold the Buddhist practice. He was so extravagant that he got into serious debt; consequently, he ran away. Actually, if he had behaved himself, he would have led a comfortable life, and the temple would not be in such a desolate shape. Prior to his misconduct, the temple had a good income. Besides owning a few acres of land, the temple also had been receiving annual offerings of oil, rice and money from nearby villages."

Then, they walked through the village. Chu-Sun's youngest son was playing in the lane. Seeing that his uncle was coming home with many friends, he ran home immediately to tell his father, who rushed out to greet the guests. Chu-Sun invited them into the living room and gave tea and tobacco to entertain the guests.

To-Ming then recounted how he had found his home village. Chu-Sun was very happy and said, "I am glad that you could find your home village. This is indeed the grace of God. Incidentally, you came at the right time too. I have a house-maid who has suffered a swollen foot for many days. Since I have been too busy, I have not found a doctor for her. Now that you are here, maybe you can help and cure her."

"I will be glad to take a look."

Chu-Sun sent for the maid. To-Ming examined her foot; indeed, it was badly swollen. He made an incision and let out the pus. That night her pain lessened. The next day she recovered quickly and could start working again.

After having dinner at Chu-Sun's house, To-Ming strolled by himself by the pond. Seeing that no one was around, he looked up to the evening sky and sighed. He then offered to God a thanksgiving prayer:

> *Father God, thank you very much indeed. From sin, You had chosen me. After leaving the home village and homeland, wandering outside for thirty years, I never expected to come back here today. And now, through Brother Chu-Sun, I finally get to come back to where I was born.*
>
> *This occasion is also the wedding of Chu-Sun's son. I had come to congratulate my friend. It turns out that others have extended congratulations to me instead. From everlasting to everlasting, who can comprehend the depth of God's grace.*
>
> *Your Word says, 'The LORD is the Father of orphans.' 'Come unto me, all you who are weary and*

heavy laden, and I will give him rest.' 'If you ask anything
in My Name, I will do it.' Father God, now I know that
you have indeed listened to the petition that I prayed day
and night for over ten years. You have allowed me to
come home. You have chosen me so that those people
who do not know you may know that it is by my Saviour
and Lord Jesus that I can come home. Holy Father, You
do fulfill your promises to those who fear You.

After praying, To-Ming returned to the living room.
Chu-Sun took him and Ou to Kap-Chuan's book room to
prepare their beds. Kap-Chuan and his father were hospitable
hosts, treating the two guests with special kindness. They also
marveled at his story of finding his home village after so many
years. They attributed this occurrence to his faith in Jesus
Christ. They talked until mid-night.

After the three Leung's retired to their bedrooms, To-Ming
and Ou knelt down to pray and to offer thanksgiving prayers
together. To-Ming was moved by Ou's sincere offering of
thanksgiving to God on his behalf. After prayers, Ou said, "It
was after our tour through your home village today that I knew
your original surname is TO. Can you tell me how you got the
surname of So?"

To-Ming replied, "I picked So twenty some years ago when
I was in America. Nevertheless, I did not tell anyone, not even
my beloved wife. As for my children, I only told them that my
father died early, and my mother remarried to another area.
I didn't tell them the details, because I knew that telling them
would only add to my sorrow. So, I just kept all the painful
past in my heart. Trusting that someday, after I find my home
village, I would tell them the details.

"In these past few years of knowing you, I have found that
you know the Way and serve our Lord. Due to your maturity,
I have always respected you. In addition, you helped me to
come back and find my home village, I am glad to share with
you all that I remember from my wretched childhood."

So To-Ming recounted his background in detail to Ou, "I started understanding things when I was very young. I even remember my father holding me in his arms. But he died very early.

"After I came to know Jesus as my Lord, my life was changed. Since the Lord Jesus has been a father to me, I just named myself after Him. That is why I had a surname of So."

To-Ming also recounted how he was able to marry a Christian woman. It amazingly worked out even though he did not have living parents nor relatives to arrange for him. Throughout this unusual marriage arrangement, his Christian friends functioned as his family and relatives.

While many marriages in China were arranged, concerned parents often tried their best to ensure that their children would have good marriages. One way of ensuring compatibility included the custom of checking the Chinese Zodiac of the potential marriage partner of their child. The Chinese Zodiac, also called "Eight Characters," stood for the eight Chinese characters for the time of birth, i.e. the year, month, day and hour of birth. This custom was based on the belief that marital happiness also depended on the compatibility of the "Eight Characters" on both sides. This custom is still practiced by some Chinese around the world.[18]

Ou thought about the prevalent practice of diagnosing the marriage fortune based on the "Eight Characters." He wondered how such practice might have affected To-Ming, who obviously would not have known his "Eight Characters." Ou asked, "Since your father-in-law was not a Christian, he must have asked for your year, month, day and hour of birth. Since you had no record of any such information, how did you handle that?"

---

[18] This superstition is gaining popularity in the western world in a modified form, as seen in the printing of zodiac in many major newspapers.

"Oh, I got my "Eight Characters" from the Bible. I just gave him the date and time of festivals in the Book of Exodus." As he got his family name from the Bible, it was natural for him to look to the Bible for birth-related information. After all, he was born into God's family through believing in Jesus.

"That was a marvelous idea." Ou exclaimed and laughed.

After the long talk, both of them retired to bed. Overwhelmed by the experience of the day, To-Ming could not fall asleep. He remained awake all night, pondering the day's events.

CHAPTER 13
The Maternal Uncle's House

On the morning of November 21, after prayers with Ou, To-Ming invited Ou to accompany him to visit his maternal uncle's home. As they approached the Leung's Ancestral Hall, To-Ming was gratified to recognize his uncle's house.

Three hundred feet away was a pond. Across the dike was the Mak's Ancestral Hall. An old banyan tree still stood across the dike. He remembered that he used to pass by this tree, where vendors set up booths for selling under the shade of this tree. Now the place was deserted. He could see his uncle's house. The stone steps on the lane by the pool were still the same. The cattle pen by the house still looked the same. Nevertheless, the few huts, his uncle's vegetable garden and the longan fruit were gone. He pointed out his maternal grandmother's house to Ou. Since he had forgotten his uncle's name, he did not go up the stone path to knock at the door.

A young man in his twenties came down the steps. To-Ming approached him and asked, "Do you happen to know the people who used to live in this house thirty years ago?"

"No, I don't. I just know that the present residents belong to the Luk family," the young man replied.

"Then do you know of the big longan tree and the vegetable garden that were here over twenty years ago?"

"No! Sorry, I don't know."

Ou and To-Ming gave up and strolled to the ancestral altar nearby. The houses and even the trees were the same as before. He remembered that many people used to buy and sell in the open space in front of the altar, just like a market place. Now the place was quiet.

Then, they walked up the altar pretending to look at the couplet written on the tablets on the side. They were using that as an opportunity to wait for some elderly people to show up so they could ask them questions. When no one came they got down and left.

A short distance from there was a small shop. An old man over sixty years old was sitting in front of the shop. They went up to him to strike up a conversation.

To-Ming bowed to him and asked, "I trust that you have good business here."

"Well, the business is pretty good. But you know that it is quite limited for a village like this. Gentlemen, where do you come from?" the old man asked.

"We came from Canton to visit Mr. Leung Chu-Sun."

"Oh, tomorrow is the wedding of Mr. Leung's son. Well, come on in and sit down. Have some tea and tobacco."

After sitting down and chatting for a short while, To-Ming asked, "During the Taiping Rebellion, the house at the top of that stone path belonged to a relative of mine. We haven't seen each other for thirty years. I am coming to pay respect to his descendants."

"Many things have changed since that time. I can't tell you everything in detail. Now the house belongs to the Luk family," the old man continued to recount a few incidents about some of the people who used to live there. To-Ming suspected that his uncle's name was mentioned, but he had no idea what it was.

"Do you know anyone who belongs to the Tong family?"

The old man pointed to the house right next to the altar. Since it did not match his uncle's house, he knew that his uncle was not of the Tong family. He also knew that the distant aunt was mistaken when she told him that his mother's maiden name was Tong. He was a little depressed because he did not know how to continue the inquiry. So, they returned to Leung's house.

CHAPTER 14
Reunion With Mother

After breakfast, the village elders sent Ting, To-Ming's paternal cousin, to visit him. Ting said, "Last night, the village elders checked the genealogy and found out that your mother's maiden name was Woo. It was not Tong, as some of the villagers said. In addition, the village elders advised you to follow tradition and register your name in the genealogy in the first month of next year."

To-Ming took the advice gladly. After a while, Ting took leave to visit his father-in-law, Tam, whose house was next to Yee-Fung's.

About an hour later, some people from the Leung family came in and announced, "Your mother is outside with her eldest sister. They are coming here to meet you."

To-Ming was astonished to hear the news. He wondered how the story about his finding his home and relatives could travel so fast.

Ou offered counsel to To-Ming, "By now, who does not know that you have come here to find your family? I am sure that the rumor about your being successful and rich has also gotten around. This is a sinful world. People may come and pretend to be your mother. I have thought of a scheme to help us discern the true one. Since all of us here are of the same age, we can all sit here first. Then, we will invite her to come in to pick out her son. In spite of many years of separation, there should still be some traces of your former appearance that she can identify."

Ou's counsel was practical and timely. All To-Ming's friends applauded his idea. They deeply respected Ou's maturity and wisdom. They arranged the seats and proceeded as Ou suggested. Then, they sent for the two women. As they were waiting, the seconds seemed like hours. All his friends were wondering what would happen. Suspense filled the room as they watched the two women being ushered into the room.

Before anyone could say a word, the woman with a bonnet pointed immediately at To-Ming and called his childhood nickname. Taken by surprise, To-Ming and all his friends rose up together. They were eager to hear the explanation for her claim. To-Ming also questioned her on how he had been separated from her, how his father had died and other details of his childhood.

Taking a deep sigh, she started her story, "When you were young, you caught smallpox. Your maternal grandmother and I had to carry you around day and night. Actually, it was quite a difficult time for you. I still remember that you had a big smallpox scar on your waist. I don't think that anyone else knows that."

Finding that all the details matched perfectly, To-Ming knew that this woman was his real mother. He felt as if his heart was being pierced. Tears welled up from his eyes, but he controlled himself so as not to cry out. He looked up and thanked God for His grace and mercy.

He then said to his mother, "We have been separated for thirty years. I am thankful that we can be reunited today. We should thank the Lord Jesus Christ because this reunion is due to His grace."

He continued, "Today is also a happy day in the Leung family. Your son came here to congratulate my host, Mr. Leung, at the wedding. As you know the culture well, you know that it is not good to cry at another family's happy occasion. Therefore, Mother, please don't cry. Otherwise, the Leung family may be displeased. When we meet another day, we can express our emotions, and share the difficult times that we had gone through. In a few days, I will be going back to Canton. I would like to invite you to come and stay with us. How do you feel about that?"

His mother remained silent for a long while and did not reply. Her eldest sister cut in and spoke on her behalf, "You have been separated for thirty years already. It is a blessing from heaven that we can meet again, and that you wish to provide for her. How can she not go? Actually, I would like to keep her company on this trip too."

"Since you are my eldest aunt, I would be pleased if you decide to accompany her. Let's set the 24th for you to depart on the boat."

His eldest aunt then asked, "How many children do you have now?"

"I have three sons and three daughters."[19]

On hearing that, people congratulated his mother. In the traditional Oriental culture, having many grandchildren was a sign of special blessing.

"I had planned to go with Mr. Ou to visit Bamboo Island Village to find Mother. How did you know that I had come back to find my roots? I am surprised you found out where I am staying." To-Ming asked his aunt.

"After you went to visit Mu Sun Lee Village yesterday, one of your distant aunts heard about it. She immediately came to tell me. I found out from Mr. Wong He-Bong where you were staying. Early this morning, I rushed to Bamboo Island Village to look for your mother. At first, she was skeptical. She didn't believe her long lost son was really here. Then others carried the same news to her. The same report, from so many different people, convinced her. She even said, 'If there is such a thing, the good Lord in Heaven must have pity on me for what I have suffered for thirty years.' That's why she agreed to come."

While they were talking, Ting came over from his in-law's house. He had heard that To-Ming had found his mother. He also wanted to meet her and witness the reunion. By this time, a big crowd of people, both young and old, had gathered outside the door. They had come to see the reunion.

---

[19] Later in 1885, To-Ming had an additional son.

At this time, Leung Chu-Sun entered the room and started to talk to To-Ming's mother. "It is the grace of our Lord that you, mother and son, are reunited."

Chu-Sun then invited To-Ming's mother and aunt to the ancestral hall for breakfast. During the meal he explained to them the way of salvation through the Lord Jesus Christ and encouraged the women to believe. After the meal, the two women went back to Bamboo Island Village.

Deeply touched by Chu-Sun's hospitality, To-Ming said, "I am very grateful for your special kindness. You have extended your hospitality not just to me, but to my mother as well."

On the same day, the news of their reunion spread far and wide. Almost all people in the neighboring villages heard the news. They marveled at the unusual way in which they had been united after such a long and difficult separation; and they attributed it to special blessings from Heaven.

CHAPTER 15
Meeting Relatives

After they got back to Leung's house, To-Ming sat down to write a letter to inform his family that he had found his mother, and that he planned to bring her back to Canton on the twenty-fifth day of the month. Just as when he wrote his previous letter to his son, he was so overwhelmed by emotions that he could not write legibly. Again, he asked Ou to write for him. The letter was as follows:

21st day of the 11th month

My dear son Ying-Fun,

I trust that you have received my previous letter describing in detail how I found my home village. On the 21st, I even met my mother at Mr. Leung's home in Yiu-Koo Village. She is not yet sixty, and still in pretty good health. I carefully questioned her on quite a few details of my life. As her answers matched all the minute details, I have no doubt that she is indeed my mother.

I am overwhelmed with emotion because of our being able to meet again after thirty years of separation. It's just like waking up from a dream. I really thank God for His abundant grace.

On the 24th, I will be departing for Canton with my mother and my eldest aunt. Please prepare a room with beds and sheets ready for them. We want to welcome them.

Remember to pray earnestly day and night and trust our Lord to keep our whole household.

Father

When the letter was finished, To-Ming had other matters to attend to. The story of his reunion with his mother was not the only information that the villagers had passed to each other. They also reported that To-Ming was a doctor. As a result, a stream of patients came to him seeking medical advice. In the afternoon, a cousin named A-Pui came to claim kinship. Seeing that he came barefooted and in ragged clothes, To-Ming asked what his job was. A-Pui answered that he did not have a trade that could provide for a stable living. They talked for almost an hour. Probably the line of patients waiting to be seen prevented A-Pui from expressing his true feelings before he left.

After he was gone, some people of the Leung's said to To-Ming, "This cousin of yours is good for nothing. He is very lazy, and addicted to opium. Having no filial piety, he mistreats his mother. That's why his mother is afraid to go home and often stays with her son-in-law." To-Ming felt very sorry to know about the true character of this cousin.

About five o'clock in the afternoon, his aunt (mother's brother's wife) came to claim kinship. She was A-Pui's mother. She recognized To-Ming immediately, and called him by his childhood nickname. As a child he had stayed frequently at his maternal grandmother's home.

They stood and talked for a long time. When Leung Yee-Fung and Leung Chu-Sun came in, To-Ming was amazed that she addressed the two Leung's as "brothers." As it was getting late, she rose to leave. To-Ming made an appointment to call on her the next day. After she left, Yee-Fung said, "Your aunt is actually my 'sister' (paternal cousin)."[20]

To-Ming was surprised to hear this new connection in kinship with the Leung family. He again expressed

---

[20] Chinese frequently address paternal cousins as brothers or sisters. Not only do they have the same surname, they often share the same generation name.

the Bible about the unsearchable grace of God. He noted in his testimony, "Who can understand the marvelous grace of God? The person He used to guide me back turns out to be my relative. I even return to my home village, and He brings my mother. He has manifested His marvelous blessings to me to confirm my faith in Him. I can see that the Lord brings His promises to pass. The Lord is indeed close to those who fear Him."

That night, Leung Kep-Chuan and his father came to chat. They also praised God that it was truly the grace of Jesus that To-Ming could find his village and mother. An hour later, Kep-Chuan's father left for bed.

Kep-Chuan then told a story about To-Ming's uncle, "The aunt that you met today is actually my cousin. When you mentioned the kindness of your uncle (her husband) and your maternal grandmother, I began to think that I am also indebted to your uncle. When I was young, I was kidnaped by bandits for a ransom of a few hundred dollars. My parents were very sad and had to agree to deliver the money to a secret location. When your uncle heard about that, he went to the bandits' den by himself, carrying a sword and a long piece of cloth. He found me and tied me to his back with the cloth. Raising their swords, the bandits tried to stop him. Your uncle fought back with his sword. The bandits were so frightened that they let him go. Thus, I was saved, and my parents did not have to pay the ransom. That is why I am always grateful to him.

"He was an unusual gentleman. He also had exceptional strength. He could lift weights of a few hundred pounds. He could fight off many people at the same time. He liked to help those who were being mistreated. Therefore, even the local tyrants dared not touch him. His name was feared and respected in this community.

"After the suppression of the Taiping Rebellion, a village elder of another clan was jealous of him. Afraid that he could not be kept under control, the village elder falsely accused him as having joined the Taiping Rebellion. That was not a true charge at all. Well, it might have been possible that during the famine, he was forced to work with the Taiping people for a living. But so were many other people, including even the local gentry. Yet, he was the only person who was falsely accused that way. The elders from the Leung clan tried to bail him out. However, the elder from the other clan said, 'We will let him go if you can guarantee that he will not harm any of us in the future.'

"The other Leung elders were familiar with your uncle's temperament. They knew that he would fight any injustice. Therefore, they dared not become guarantors for him. So, he was executed under false charges. I heard that the person who framed him has no living descendants, probably due to this grave iniquity of being a false witness."

To-Ming sighed deeply after hearing that his uncle had died in such dishonor, and in such an undeserving way. They talked till early morning. Before retiring, Ou and To-Ming knelt down together to pray, thanking God again for the way He had led To-Ming to his home village and to his mother and other relatives.

Even though his body was in bed, To-Ming could not sleep again. His mind wandered through the difficult and joyful experiences in the past thirty years. He stayed awake until the birds started chirping outside the window. Still in his bed, he decided to offer his prayer of thanksgiving to God.

CHAPTER 16
Christian Wedding At The Village

On the morning of the 22nd, To-Ming told Ou that he could not sleep the whole night. Ou replied, "It is only natural that you are overwhelmed by such special times of sorrow and joy."

They had their morning prayer together. Then, they went to congratulate Chu-Sun, for today was his son's wedding day. Afterward, they went to visit To-Ming's aunt.

In front of his aunt's house, they were pleasantly surprised by seeing his aunt and other relatives coming out to greet them. They went into the Luk's family greeting room. A cousin of To-Ming's mother, Kai-Ming, said, "I can't believe that we can meet again like this."

His aunt wept as she said, "Since your uncle's death, our family has gone through difficult times. I can't tell you how much I have suffered in all these years."

To-Ming had some questions for his aunt. "When did my Po-Po die?"

"She died more than ten years ago. Since her death, our family went through still more difficult times. Your cousin did not behave himself. Then, he was kidnaped and almost shipped to be a laborer abroad. Fortunately, we found out early enough. So we sold the old big house as ransom to claim him back."

To-Ming had fond memories of how his Po-Po had cared for him. At that time, Po-Po's family was rather well-off. Seeing that her family had changed to such a sad condition, and that his beloved Po-Po was gone, To-Ming sighed deeply and said, "It is really by the grace of the Lord Jesus that I am able to return to my home village, and see all the relatives. I am not returning as a rich man. Knowing that you are in difficulty, I don't know what is the best way to help.

Nevertheless, would you consider coming with us to live in Canton? What do you think?"

His aunt replied, "I cannot come now. However, I would certainly come and visit in the first month of next year."

After an hour, they left to go back to Chu-Sun's house for breakfast. At noon, Chu-Sun sent the sedan out to the bride's village to pick-up the bride, as part of the traditional Chinese custom of welcoming the bride into the bridegroom's household. Preparing for the bride's arrival, the band began to play, colorful banners were displayed and fire crackers were lighted, signifying a lively and joyous occasion.

While they were waiting in the afternoon, many sick people came from neighboring villages to To-Ming for treatment. About five in the evening, the bride arrived. A crowd gathered outside to watch.

That night, the banquet hall was filled with people for the celebration. They feasted and ate until they were filled before departing. About 8 P.M., Chu-Sun invited Ou and To-Ming to his house for prayer with the new couple. The house was packed with people to witness the occasion.

Ou started the meeting[21] by explaining from the Bible principles regarding the husband-wife relationship. He then led them to sing a few hymns of praise. Afterward, he prayed for blessings on the new couple, that they would abide by God's truth all life long. Then, Chu-Sun also prayed and blessed his son and daughter-in-law that they might fear the Lord.

---

[21] Since becoming a Christian in 1864, Ou was known for his faith and zealous service. His wide reading in Chinese literature complemented well with his knowledge of Scriptural truth. Recognizing his gifts, the London Missionary Society used him in translating the Bible, editing commentaries, and overseeing a church in Hong Kong. In that church he had a reputation of clearly explaining the Scriptures. It must be for these reasons that the Leung family invited him to conduct the wedding.

After the ceremony, they went back to Kep-Chuan's book room. They talked some more, almost until midnight. Before going to bed, Ou and To-Ming prostrated themselves to pray. Just like the night before, To-Ming was overwhelmed with emotion. He could not fall asleep all night. At daybreak, he just sat up in his bed and prayed.

CHAPTER 17
Testimony And Banquet For Village Elders

On the 23rd, after morning devotions with Ou, To-Ming and Ou took a walk to the hill near the house. Attracted by the scenery of the few dozen old pine trees on the hill, Ou invited To-Ming to climb the hilltop for a panoramic view.

They walked up a winding path to the foot of the hill, but they could not find the trail up the hill. Fortunately, they met an old woman who pointed them to the correct trail about thirty feet ahead. Following her directions, they went up a narrow rugged trail overgrown with trees. With the help of the vines, they climbed to the hilltop.

The hilltop was rather flat. They saw a few old tombs overgrown with weeds. They found out that these were the tombs of the forefathers of the Leung clan in the area. In the midst of the tombs was an old pine tree. From the color of the bark they thought that the tree must be a few hundred years old. Ou said, "This tree reminds me of the poem from the Tang Dynasty, 'A pine tree grows to look like the scales of an old dragon.' I guess people in those ancient days did have amazing insight."

After an hour or so, they searched for the trail to go downhill. Due to the steep slope, the descent was more difficult. They held onto the vines with their hands to go down. When they got to the foot of the hill, they saw a few sick women waiting for treatment already. Soon many more patients came to be treated by To-Ming.

About 10 A.M, Chu-Sun came to invite Ou and To-Ming to attend a banquet prepared for the village elders. Before the food was set out, Chu-Sun bade his son and daughter-in-law to stand on the doorsteps of the ancestral hall. Ou delivered a message on the biblical teaching concerning union in matrimony, the God who created the heavens and the earth, and the way of redemption for man through Jesus Christ. He also urged people to forsake false gods and to trust in Jesus, to worship the one and eternal living God. His message lasted about an hour.

After the message, Chu-Sun exhorted the new couple with more biblical teaching. Then, he invited Ou and To-Ming to sing a hymn of praise. After the duet, Chu-Sun gave a closing prayer, including a supplication for the people's receptivity to the gospel.

The banquet started at noon. To-Ming overheard some people saying that they would rather listen to the gospel than have the good food, for they rarely had opportunities to hear such a meaningful message.

Their receptivity was indeed outstanding during this time, since Christianity was still considered a foreign religion by most Chinese. Additionally, Christians constituted a tiny minority in China, especially in the villages. The good reception was probably attributed to Ou's ability to expound biblical teaching in the context of Chinese culture. The Leung family also contributed to the good reception of the gospel by having established good rapport and earned the respect of the local residents. They were successful in communicating the Christian message through the traditional customs.

In the afternoon, To-Ming invited Ou to tour the farms and the ditches, and the temple in front of the village. That night, they again chatted until very late at night. As was their habit, Ou and To-Ming knelt down to pray before going to bed. Just like the last few nights, To-Ming's mind was filled with the events of the past few days. He slept only for a couple of hours.

CHAPTER 18
Homeward Bound With Mother

On the morning of the 24th, after morning devotions with Ou, To-Ming and Ou received an invitation to have breakfast with one of the Leung's elders, Hel-Tong's father. After breakfast, they began their journey home. Chu-Sun and his brothers saw them off to the gate of the village.

To-Ming and Ou then walked to the dock by the river. To-Ming's mother and his aunt were already sitting in front of the temple, waiting for them. Accompanying them on the boat were his uncle Kai-Ming and cousin A-Pui.

The boat set sail at noon. The route was similar to the way they came, passing places like Fu-San. They arrived in Canton on the morning of the 25th. They hired a small boat to go ashore near the Sandbar Gospel Church. To-Ming asked Ou to stay with his mother and aunt, while he went home to tell his family to get ready to welcome them. Ou consented.

When To-Ming returned to the church, Ou already had left with To-Ming's mother and aunt. To-Ming returned to his home, but Ou was gone already. To-Ming's wife said, "Ou brought your mother here, and left for his own home. I invited him to stay for breakfast. Yet, he said that he should return to his home first."

To-Ming was deeply touched by Ou's love for him, and the care shown to his mother. He also appreciated Ou for being such a good companion and wise counsel on this trip.

Meanwhile, To-Ming's father-in-law and his relatives arrived for the reunion celebration. His wife greeted each of the relatives by serving tea according to the Chinese tradition. The tea ceremony was an expression of respect for older relatives, especially to the parents. Usually, the tea ceremony was performed shortly after a wedding, or the first time the bride met the parents.[22]

His wife had also ordered a banquet to celebrate his fruitful return. That night, they invited quite a few relatives for the joyous celebration. His relatives congratulated him for finding his home and his mother.

After prayer, To-Ming told his mother, "It is by the grace of our Lord Jesus that we can be reunited. I will be glad to care for you. I hope that you can just stay here and not return to Bamboo Island."

She replied, "I have been there for over thirty years. I have many ties there. There is no way for me to cut off my ties like that."

Hearing that she had a strong desire to go back, he knew that he could not insist that she stay with him. However, he did hope that his mother might come to know and trust in Jesus Christ.

On the same day, Ou had spread the good news of To-Ming's dramatic return to his home village to all the churches in Canton. Later, the news even spread to churches in the surrounding counties and Hong Kong. As a result, all people who knew To-Ming heard about the story. They rejoiced with him and attributed the special blessings to be from the Father.

The incident was also a pleasant surprise to the pastor of the First Presbyterian Church in Canton. The pastor was happy to see To-Ming bring his mother to church and offer his thanksgiving to God. That Sunday morning, Rev. Happer asked To-Ming to share his story with the whole congregation.

To-Ming started by giving a brief summary of his difficult childhood. "I suffered much as an orphan. For many years, I

---

[22] The tea ceremony still continues among overseas Chinese as a way to honor parents. Quite often, it has been modified for the newly wed couple to serve tea to parents of both bridegroom and bride in their respective household.

wandered through many different places, even across the ocean to America. Later, by the grace of God, I came to know the gospel and believed.

"After I became a Christian, I prayed earnestly every day that God would guide me back to my home village, to see my mother. Thirty years later, God answered my prayer.

"The Bible says, 'Our Lord God is a Father to orphans' and 'Call unto me, I will answer you.' Our Lord Jesus also said, 'If you ask anything in my name, I will do it.' I now truly appreciate that God indeed answers prayers.

"Brothers and sisters, if you have worries, you can pray just like I did. As you pray without ceasing, you will experience His comfort and peace. Now, I don't want you to think that He will immediately grant your prayers. Sometimes, He may withhold the answer to your requests to test our faith.

"According to Mark 7:14-30, Jesus went to the regions of Tyre and Sidon, where He met a Syrophoenician woman. She asked Jesus to heal her daughter. Our Lord said, '…it is not good to take the children's bread and throw it to the dogs.' What does that mean? Actually, our Lord already knew her heart. She had the faith that Jesus was able to heal. Jesus was just testing her faith and humility. Our Lord used her as an example for us, so that we too can learn to ask in faith. When we ask, we should have sincere faith, and have the patience to wait. Just like this woman, God may grant our request if we pray in His time, which may be soon or later. Sometimes, it is only after we receive His blessings that we realize His divine plan and purpose. The purpose of His timing may be to protect us, to teach us, to lead us into deeper understanding of His truth, or to appreciate His abounding grace.

"Brethren, be steadfast in your prayers. When you have prayed many times and still do not see results, do not lose faith. We should follow the example of that Syrophoenician woman and ask in faith."

The next day, Rev. Happer invited To-Ming to his home to inquire about the details of To-Ming's childhood and how he was kidnaped. So To-Ming again recounted his experiences and how he had prayed for thirty years. He also shared how God had used the hands of the Leung brothers, members of the same local church, to guide him back. Furthermore, he shared how he was amazed to find that the Leungs came from the same village and were distant cousins.

Later, the account of To-Ming's return was put into the bulletins of many churches in areas surrounding Canton.

CHAPTER 19
Register In The Family Tree

A new name plate was put up in front of To-Ming's office. Dr. SO's Office became Dr. TO's Office. His whole household also changed their surname to TO.

Later, he made many trips back to his home village. He did quite a few things according to the tradition of the clan and the contemporary custom of the land.

In the first month of the ninth year when Kuang-Hsu was the emperor (1883), he officially registered his wife and his three sons in the family tree of his clan. Thus, he became associated with a clan that had a genealogy that went back for many generations.

Through these trips, he found out more information about his childhood. There were many interesting encounters with village elders. One time, a village elder who was familiar with his relatives said to him, "You were lost and gone for thirty years, and then you were able to find your roots and home village. I think it is attributable to the protection of your ancestors' spirits."

"Not really!" To-Ming responded. "If I did not trust in our Lord Jesus Christ, I don't think that I would have even learned to pray and have been able to see the answers to prayers. Then, I would not get to see all of you." To-Ming took the opportunity to explain the Christian gospel for almost half an hour.

The same elder also recounted what happened after To-Ming was kidnapped, "Your kidnapping was the fault of your uncle and aunt who did not fulfill their family responsibilities. After your disappearance, some elders rebuked your uncle and said, 'You have only one nephew. You should have cared for him even during hard times. You should not have let him suffer like that.'

"Your uncle replied that he did not know. He blamed his wife and beat her several times. He even went to argue with your maternal grandmother, accusing her of abducting you. He did all that to cover up his faults. Later his wife died without any offspring. He later remarried and had a son. He died at the age of sixty, leaving no money behind. They had to sell your house to a cousin to get money to bury him. Later his son died too. With nothing to depend on, his wife married into another family.

"People in the clan often wondered how your grandfather, Elder TO Kwong-Tai, who was such a nice man, could end up with no descendants to carry on the family name? He had three sons and one daughter. They were all married, but you were his only grandchild. That was why he loved you so much.

"After your father died, Elder Kwong-Tai, your grandfather, selected the site for the tomb. He claimed to know *Feng-Shui*. He also explained that the soil was very good. He said to the relatives, 'I am poor now. Yet with my son being buried in this good soil, his descendants will get rich. Also, based on the Eight Characters, the time of my grandson's birth was very good. If he had been born in the provinces near the imperial capital in Northern China, he could have become a high ranking government official.'

"People often talked about what Elder Kwong-Tai said about the fate of his descendant. They said that he was wrong in his predictions. However, they never expected that you would come back. So, I guess that he was right after all."

To-Ming replied, "Whether we become rich or poor is not because of the kind of land for burial or the time of birth. All blessings come from God. My grandfather never heard of the true way. That was why he talked about *Feng-Shui* and the Eight Characters. Actually, these two things do not even fit Confucius' teachings."

They continued talking on such topics until midnight.

Between 1883 and 1887, he took a few more trips back to the village to repair his ancestors' graves. On some of the trips, he took his eldest son with him to oversee the repair work. The reconstructions were needed to rectify the deplorable situation of the grave sites. Since there were no immediate relatives around, the grave sites were overgrown with weeds and unsightly. He also put up some marble tombstones.

Some of his trips were delayed and interrupted by the French invasions of China. Nevertheless, he kept on returning. On these trips, he always brought medicine with him. Therefore, whenever local villagers heard about his returning, word would spread quickly around the villages. Because of his kindness and care, he was always well received. He was often swarmed by people seeking medical treatment. Sometimes, people traveled for miles to come for treatment. At times, people followed him all the way to the boat. Even a few days after he had left the village, people would travel to his village, thinking that he was still there. As a result of these trips, many people from the villages around the area heard his story. Furthermore, he had many opportunities to explain the gospel of Jesus Christ.

Like the Hebrew culture, the Chinese were careful in maintaining the record of their genealogy. To-Ming wrote the genealogy of the TO family, tracing the names of ancestors back five more generations. This was probably one of the few Chinese genealogies with a distinct Christian perspective. The genealogy began with the following words of thanksgiving:

> *"I am deeply grateful for the two Leung brothers, Yee-Fung and Chu-Sun, who brought me back to my home village and my kinsfolk. On the 20th day of the 11th month, 1881, I found my home village. On the 21th day, I found my own mother. During the years of famine, I was separated from my mother. For about thirty years, I went through many difficult years. Now I can be*

*reunited with my mother, and trace my genealogy. I
attribute all these to the grace of God."*

Thus, he fulfilled all the expectations on the Chinese of his
day. He returned to his home village, paid respect and
provided care for his living mother, repaired his ancestors'
graves, registered in the family tree of the village and updated
the genealogy. As a Christian, however, he went further in
sharing with others the grace of God.

To help his descendants appreciate the grace of God, he
wrote his personal testimony, naming it *The Story of My
Homecoming*. It presented how he lived through his difficult
childhood, how he became a Christian and how he found his
home village and mother. Since the account was intended for
his family, he included some of his personal feelings, his
prayers, and two of his letters. Like typical documents of his
day, it was written in classical Chinese. His story presented his
deep gratitude to God and people who helped him. It began
with the following words:

> *The Bible says, "…God causes all things to work
> together for good to those who love God, to those who are
> called according to his purpose." (Romans 8:28)*
> *I will always be indebted to the Leung brothers,
> Chu-Sun and Yee-Fung, for guiding me back to my home
> village and helping me find my mother.*

To share with his posterity, he gave a copy of the "TO
Genealogy" and his homecoming account to each of his four
sons. The documents were meticulously hand copied in good
calligraphy with Chinese brush. He requested his children and
grandchildren to share them with their descendants.

EPILOGUE

Jesus Christ offers hope for the world. Throughout the ages, people from all lands have experienced the special abundant life that He offers. This book is the story of changed lives and Christians who made the difference.

A few words should be said about two people who were good friends of the main character in this story. Mr. Leung Chu-Sun helped the London Missionary Society in establishing churches. Later, he served in a church south of Canton.

Mr. Ou Fung-Chee (1847-1914) appeared to be an excellent companion for Dr. TO To-Ming's trip back to the home village. The writer and other readers were deeply impressed by his wise and timely counsel, his leadership, his devout faith and witness, and his being such a good friend. He appeared to be a recognized Christian leader. He officiated the two Christian ceremonies at the village.

Research showed that Mr. Ou made his mark in his service for the kingdom of God and the Republic of China. He served as an elder of a London Missionary Society church in Hong Kong. In 1883, he became a teacher of young Sun Yat-Sen, who later became the founding father of the Republic of China. Besides tutoring him in Chinese literature, he gave Sun the name "Yat-Sen," which Dr. Sun was known by around the world.[23] Furthermore, he introduced Sun to the American missionary, Charles R. Hager who baptized Sun in 1883. After finishing medical training in the Canton Christian Hospital and the Hong Kong Medical College, Dr. Sun traveled around the world to organize the overthrow of the corrupt Ching Dynasty. In 1896, on his way to church in London, Dr. Sun was abducted

---

[23] James S. Cha, "Ou Fung-Chee" Ch. 9 *Concise Biographies of Important Chinese Christians* China Evangelical Seminary Press, Taipei, 1982, pp. 45-48.

by agents of the Ching Regime and detained secretly within the Chinese (Ching Dynasty) Embassy for over ten days. After being rescued by James Cantile in London in 1896, Dr. Sun wrote a long letter to Mr. Ou describing how he prayed in captivity, how he was rescued and how his faith was strengthened in the trial.[24] The letter showed that Dr. Sun Yat-Sen deeply respected Mr. Ou.

The main character, Dr. TO To-Ming was born on 25th August, 1846. After he became a Christian in San Francisco, he took on the surname of SO. He was baptized at the age of sixteen. After he found his home village and mother in 1882, he changed his surname from SO back to TO.

For many years, Dr. TO To-Ming continued to practice medicine in his office on the Western Section of Canton. For one or two days a week, he taught medicine in the Canton Christian (Pok-Chee) Hospital. He also gave free treatment to poor people one day a week.

In the 1880's, he played a key role in the building of the Second Presbyterian Church in Canton. That church was later renamed the Fung-Yuen Christian Church after relocation to Fung-Yuen Road. This was the church that the writer attended as a small child.

To-Ming did two things that directly influenced his descendants. As the patriarch of the TO family, he gave generation names to three generations of descendants. The writer's generation name, Yan, meaning "grace," stands for the grace of God. My parents added Pui, meaning "abundant," to complete my Chinese first name, which intends to signify "the abundant grace of God."

To-Ming's personal writings, "The Story of My Homecoming" and the "TO Genealogy" also influenced his

---

[24] Chih-Hsin Wang, *History of Christianity in China*, Chinese Christian Literature Council, Hong Kong, 3rd ed. 1979 pp. 262-63. Unfortunately, few people know the positive influence of Christianity in Dr. Sun's life and work.

descendants. One set of the two original copies was given to my grandfather, his fifth son, who was a dentist. The documents were then passed along to his eldest son, my uncle, who was also a medical doctor in Canton. His family destroyed the original copies during the Cultural Revolution. This family suffered much persecution for their Christian faith. During that period, many homes were searched carefully for anything that belonged to the past generations. There was no need to be caught in possession of such documents, which would cause additional persecution. Fortunately, a relative hand copied a set and sent them to my parents, and my mother hand copied a set for me.

Dr. TO To-Ming died on the 8th of May in 1919, 11 P.M. His wife died in 1932. They were both buried in the Christian Cemetery on Pok Fu Lam Road on Hong Kong Island.

To-Ming had four sons and three daughters, twenty-seven grandchildren, hundreds of great grandchildren and over a thousand great-great-grand children. His descendants are spread out in many countries around the world. Hopefully, they will all get to know this precious legacy from Dr. TO To-Ming.

BACKGROUND RESOURCES IN ADDITION TO FAMILY DOCUMENTS

IN ENGLISH:

Beck, William A. & David A. William, *California—A History of the Golden State*. Doubleday , 1972

Cheng, J. C., *Taiping Rebellion 1850-1864*. Hong Kong University Press, Hong Kong, 1963.

Chow, Moses C., *Reconciling Our Kinsmen in The Gold Mountain*. Ambassadors for Christ Inc., Washington D.C., 1972.

Dicker, Laverne Mau, *The Chinese in San Francisco, A Pictorial History*. Dover Publications, Inc. New York, 1979.

Hong Kong Annual Report, 1962. Hong Kong Government Press.

Latourette, Kenneth S., *Christianity in a Revolutionary Age*. vol. 3. Zondervan, 1961.

Latourette, K. S., *The Chinese, Their History and Culture*. Macmillan, New York 1962.

Pollock, J.C., *Hudson Taylor and Maria, Pioneers in China*. Zondervan, 1962.

IN CHINESE:

Cha, James S. C., "Ou Fung-Chee" Ch. 9, *Concise Biographies of Important Chinese Christians*. China Evangelical Seminary Press, Taiwan, 1983.

Tang, Christopher, *The First Hundred Years of Protestant Mission in China*. Dao Sheng Publishing House, Hong Kong 1987.

Wang, Chih-Hsin, *History of Christianity in China*, 3rd ed. Chinese Christian Literature Council, Hong Kong. 1979.

Wong, Kei-Tin, *A History of the Chinese-American Presbyterian Missionary Society, 1871-1971*. pub. n.p.

BILINGUAL:

School Bulletin, Sun Yat-Sen University of Medical Sciences, Canton, 1985.

APPENDIX

Ming Dynasty 1368 - 1643 A.D.

List of Emperors of the Ching Dynasty 1644 - 1911 A.D.

Shun Che	1644 - 1661
K'ang He	1662 - 1722
Yung Cheng	1723 - 1735
Chieng Lung	1736 - 1796
Tao Kuang	1821 - 1850
Hsien Feng	1851 - 1861
Tung Che	1862 - 1874
Kuang Hsu	1875 - 1908
Hsuen Tung	1909 - 1911

List of Photographs, Sketches, and Maps

1. Dr. TO To-Ming

2. **Dr. TO To-Ming's wife, Pong**

3. Tombstone of Dr. TO To-Ming in Hong Kong

4. Tree at entrance of Mu Sun Lee Village where To-Ming was kidnapped. Early 1900's.

5. Tree at entrance of Mu Sun Lee Village in 1988

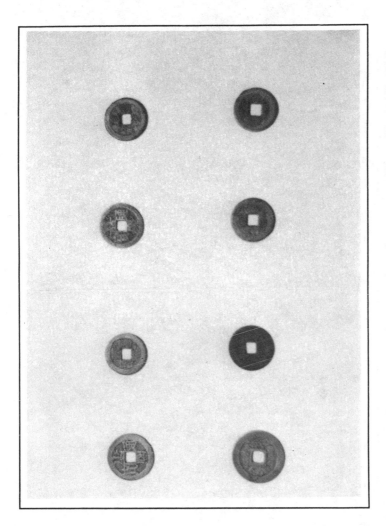

6. Copper coins minted during the reign of emperors: K'ang He (1662-1722), Yung Cheng (1723-1735), Chieng Lung (1736-1796), Tao Kuang (1821-1850)

7. Chinese sign saying "Yam Tong," referring to a church hall. San Francisco, 19th Century.

Photo Source: *The Chinese in San Francisco,* Laverne Mau Dicker, used by permission from Dover Publications, New York

8. Chinese Church Hall in San Francisco, 19th Century, with sign "Foke Yam Tong" (Gospel Hall)

Photo Source: *The Chinese in San Francisco*, Laverne Mau Dicker, used by permission from Dover Publications, New York

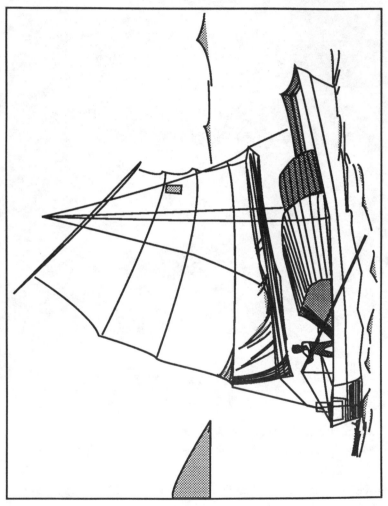

9. Sketch of a Chinese junk

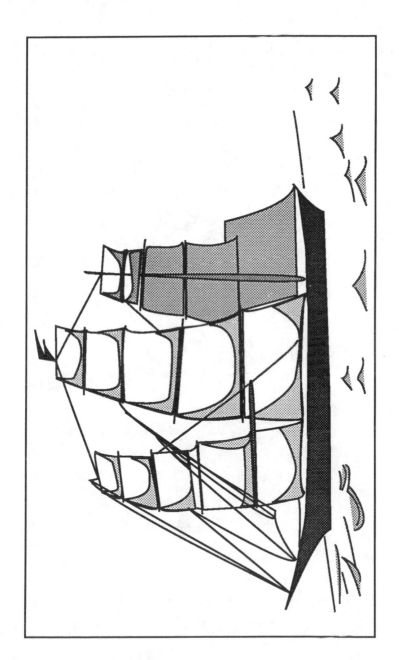

10. Sketch of a boat that crossed the Pacific Ocean in the late 1800's

11. Sketch of a Chinese houseboy, 19th Century

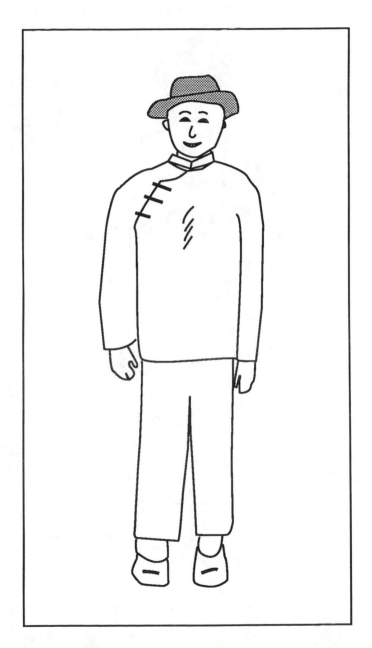

12. Sketch of 19th Century Chinese clothing worn in San Francisco

13. Sketch of 19th Century Western-style clothing worn in San Francisco

14. Gateway to Chinatown, San Francisco, with words of Dr. Sun Yat-Sen hanging from Arch, 1989

15. Stockton Street, San Francisco, 1989

16. Chinese Baptist Church on Stockton Street, San Francisco, 1989

17. Chinese Presbyterian Church on Stockton Street, San Francisco, 1989

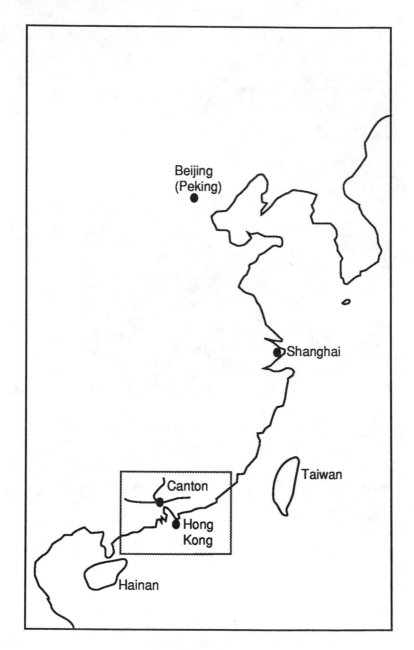

18. Map of East China